Praise for John Weagly

"I love pleasant surprises and, in this business, one of the best pleasant surprises is finding evidence of a new writer worth reading and following."

— **Edward Bryant**, *Locust Magazine*

"Exuberant."

— *Chicago Tribune*

"Appealingly quirky."

— *Chicago Sun-Times*

"Rarely loses sight of the effectiveness of well crafted prose."

— *New City*

Dancing in the Knee-Deep Midnight

a collection of short stories

by John Weagly

Close To The Bone Publishing

First published in Great Britain in 2022 by Close To The Bone

ISBN 979-8-84131-912-2

Close To The Bone
an imprint of Gritfiction Ltd
Rugby
Warwickshire
CV21
www.close2thebone.co.uk

Cover and Interior Design by Craig Douglas

First Printing, 2022

Contents

Dancing in the Knee-Deep Midnight

Terry Tenderloin and the Pig Thief

"This is about the pig," I said.

Daniel nodded. "Terry Tenderloin."

Daniel Sampson and I had just arrived at a Cape-Cod style farmhouse on the outskirts of Currie Valley. The off-yellow two-story home was on the smallish side, but had a large back yard surrounded by an American-Dream white picket fence. The aromas of a farm in full bloom filled the air - chemical spray, rotting vegetation, fresh-cut hay and animal excrement. It was early-October cool, but I could feel sweat clinging to my body.

"Nice place," I said.

"Head around to the back."

Daniel had picked me up outside of Taco Bell and asked me if I wanted to go for a ride. I politely said no and he politely showed me the pistol he had in his pocket.

"Mr. Walden has grown quite attached to Terry," Daniel said as we walked.

Pigs make great pets. A normal Vietnamese Pot-Bellied Pig can go for as much as a thousand dollars. I sold them for less than half that.

I turned to Daniel. "It's good that Mr. Walden loves Terry, right? People are supposed to get attached to their pets."

Daniel nudged me along. "It isn't good. Terry Tenderloin was the cutest thing ever when Mr. Walden brought him home, but he kept growing and growing and growing. Now, rather than having a cute little pig, Mr.

Walden has a full grown, three-hundred-and-twenty-eight pound hog."

I tried giving him my most sympathetic face. "Your boss can't blame me for that - pigs grow, they get bigger, baby pigs turn into adult pigs."

"Terry should've reached maybe a hundred pounds. You know that."

He was right.

When I learned about the money in Pot-Bellied Pigs, I decided to take advantage of the open market. I stole normal, newborn pigs from area farms and then sold them as Pot-Bellies at cut-rate prices. I only did it a few times, four-hundred dollars here and there to help tide me over. Jeremy Walden, Currie Valley's reigning crime lord, was one of those times.

"Mr. Walden loves that pig," Daniel said. "But living in a condo downtown, it's crowded. And the neighbors don't like it - him taking this hog up and down in the elevator every time Terry has to go outside to go for a walk, the smells, the noises. Luckily, Mr. Walden has money. He was able to buy this place."

I looked around at the house, the land, the beautiful, little fence. "All of this is for a pig?"

"All of this is for a valued member of the family."

We came to the back yard and there, in a patch of mud, stood Terry Tenderloin - Mr. Jeremy Walden's pet pig. He had dirty pink skin with mottled black spots, a fair amount of shit on his underside and legs and enough blubber to feed an entire Knights of Columbus picnic. He was a no-doubt-about-it full-grown hog.

"Go over and say hi," Daniel said. "And sorry about the stink, he hasn't had his bath today."

I walked over to Terry, trying to not get too much slime on my shoes. I cautiously scratched the swine between the ears, feeling his short, bristly hair. He seemed happy.

"Why did you bring me out here," I asked as I stroked the pig.

"To make amends."

"Great!" I said with relief. "Let's make this right! What do you want me to do?"

For an answer Daniel took out his gun and shot me twice, once in each kneecap. Terry Tenderloin squealed and ran from the blasts. The pain was like lightning and fire and a thousand knives. I fell to the ground and tried to scream, but all that came out were sobbing, high-pitched moans.

"The cost of food for a full-grown hog is astronomical," Daniel said. "Mr. Walden came up with this idea to help alleviate that cost."

One little scam and I'm pig groceries.

After a moment, Terry Tenderloin came back over to me, snuffling and grunting. He nudged me a couple of times with his snout, then tugged on the sleeve of my shirt.

And then dinner began.

The Resurrection at Hasenpfeffer Field

"Why did you go away?"

"I did something bad."

The two of us were in the parking lot of the Currie Valley Airport, also known as Hampstead Field – 'a little airstrip for a little town.' The terminal was a small, round building with one set of doors, one ticket counter, and one restaurant – the Hippity-Hop Cafe. Outside, there was a parking lot, a hangar and a runway. If you wanted to book a flight through Currie Valley Air, you could fly to St. Louis. That was it, St. Louis. Otherwise you could charter a plane.

"Why did you do something bad?" Cheyenne asked.

We'd talked about this before, but she always had more questions. "I needed money," I said. "For me and your Mom. And you."

"So you did something bad? For money?"

"I didn't think it was that bad. I thought I could get away with it."

Confusion crossed Cheyenne's six-year-old face. "But you didn't get away with it."

"No, I didn't."

"If you got away with it, would it still've been bad?"

"Yes."

I'd been out for almost a month and was trying to connect with her. She'd been born while I was away. Earlier that day, I'd asked her, "What would you like more than anything in the world?"

"A bunny."

"Then we'll go to the pet store and get you a bunny."

She shook her head. "An airport bunny."

Despite its modest needs, Hampstead Field took up a fair amount of terrain and most of it was grassland. Rabbits dominated the area. When flying in, you could see rabbit holes dotted all over the property. Around dusk, you could see dozens upon dozens of brown bunnies eating in the vicinity.

Because of all the rabbits, people around town called the airport Hasenpfeffer Field.

"How do you know about the bunnies at the airport?" I asked.

"Mommy takes me sometimes," Cheyenne said. "We visit the bunnies and eat supper and watch the little planes take off. There are lots of people going away."

I locked the car and we walked to the large meadow in front of the terminal. I'd brought a fishnet that once hung as a wall decoration and a cardboard box with holes punched in the lid. We stepped off the tarmac and the grass under my feet felt unfamiliar.

"Let's go slow," I said.

"Okay," Cheyenne whispered.

We inched our way toward seven rabbits relaxing in the sunset. "By the way," I said. "Do you know how you catch a unique bunny?" I'd looked this up on the internet for the occasion.

Cheyenne looked apprehensive. "No."

"Unique up on it."

She didn't laugh, or even smile. I wondered if she knew it was a joke.

"Do you know how you catch a tame bunny?" I tried.

She shook her head.

"Tame way."

No reaction. I could hear metal clanging on metal coming from the hangar. We moved on quietly.

The rabbits looked content; some of them eating, some just sitting. I noticed one with his ears back, scratching himself with one of his hind feet. He seemed to be where he wanted to be; I didn't like the idea of putting him in a cage, taking him away from his home. But I'd made a promise to my daughter, so I lifted the net, readying it for a throw. Cheyenne tip-toed behind me. As we took our time getting close, before I could even think about throwing the net, the rabbits scattered. One second they were there, the next just empty grass.

"What happened?" Cheyenne asked.

I lowered my arms, the net hitting the tops of my feet. "I'm sorry, Honey."

"Where did they all go?"

"I'm sorry." I considered trying to get one out of one of the holes and into the box, but the thought of grabbing onto wriggling fur and yanking a creature out of its life made my throat feel tight. "I don't think… I don't think I can…"

My daughter smiled at me. "It's okay, Daddy. I still got to see them. I've never gotten this close to the bunnies before."

"Okay," I said.

We walked back to the parking lot. When my feet again touched the asphalt, I felt a little more comfortable. I looked around at the cars scattered in front of the terminal. "There are lots of people going away," I said.

"Maybe there are lots of people coming back," Cheyenne said. She put her hand in mine and we walked to our car.

Lucky

"I see a wedding in your future."

Jeff almost asked the fortune teller for his money back. A wedding? For the King of the One Night Stand? Ridiculous! He'd come to Venice Beach to get lucky. Everyone said Venice girls were easy, and easy was his style. Having his palm read was just a way to pass the time until he found his next temporary girlfriend.

Now it looked like the sidewalk prophet was right.

Lisa had been sunbathing, wearing a bikini that looked like it would barely fit a six-year-old, and he knew she was tonight's main event.

"I like you a whole lot," she told him on the beach. "I'd really like to get to know you better, a whole lot better, but that involves things I can only do with the man I marry. I'm a good girl."

Jeff looked at her. Her lips. Her eyes. Her body. They all added up to one thing.

"Marry me," he blurted out. "Marry me tonight! We can be husband and wife by the time the sun goes down."

Lisa answered him with a smile. He was in luck. They drove to Las Vegas, leaving the tattoo artists, T-shirt stands and tarot cards of Venice Beach behind.

Four and a half hours from first date to honeymoon. Getting laid wasn't supposed to be this simple!

The ceremony was cheap and easy.

"Do you?"

"I do."

"Do you?"

"I do too."

Hopefully ditching her in the morning would also be cheap and easy.

The hotel was called the Honeymooners Lodge. The room had a heart-shaped bed with heart-shaped pillows. Red carpet. Red curtains. And a red, kidney-shaped bathtub. It was the last place real newly-weds would want to spend their honeymoon.

"Why don't you make yourself comfortable," Lisa said as soon as they checked in. "I'll go in the bathroom and get ready."

Jeff got undressed and climbed into bed.

And waited.

And thought about lingerie.

And waited.

And thought about skin.

And waited.

After an eternity, Lisa came out. No lingerie. No new bits of tantalizing skin. She looked exactly the same.

Except for the gun in her hand.

"I'm sorry, baby," she said.

"I... I don't have any money," Jeff said.

"It's not about money," Lisa said, "Jake is loaded."

"Jake?"

"My fiancé."

"You're engaged?"

"I was in Venice to have my tea leaves read. Madame Zora looked into my future and said I was going to be married."

"To Jake."

"Right. She also said my first husband was going to die right after our wedding."

"Jake?"

"No, honey," Lisa said. "Jake's the love of my life. I can't bear the thought of losing him."

"So you made me your first husband."

She smiled.

"But..." Jeff said, "You can't...I just...I like you a whole lot..."

"I'm sorry, baby. I like you too," Lisa said as she raised the gun, "It's just not your lucky day."

Long Distance Rumbles

Trains rumbled through my head.

I could feel them bore into my ear, crunching through the bone so they could get into my skull. Then they would hammer through my brain, hitting each out-of-the-way switching station that existed in my cerebellum. They'd screech. They'd smash. They'd splinter. Finally, when the passing was finished, they would exit my other ear. Then I would have eight minutes of silence, eight minutes until the next train came crashing through like a bullet.

***

In early April, in the eight hundred block of Chicago Avenue, I found a pistol. It was in an alley, behind a dumpster, in a puddle of rain.

I was walking, collecting job applications. I took a shortcut. The sun was out, but it had stormed the night before and puddles still marked the city here and there. A block away, an elevated train rumbled. I noticed the handle of the gun behind the Dumpster's wheel.

April showers can bring whatever you want them to bring.

When I got home, I looked inside the gun, cracked it open. One bullet was missing.

Here's what I think happened:

Someone was running from something, a robbery or a murder, and they wanted to get rid of evidence. They threw the gun away and kept running.

And I found it.

The city can be a scary place. There are a lot of people and you don't know who they are or what they're up to. A gun can be a good thing to have.

***

Through rumbles I heard ringing.

My phone was an old, red one that ringed instead of beeped. It hadn't been hooked up for very long. "Hello?" I said from the other side of half-closed eyes.

"Were you asleep?" the voice said. It was female.

"No." I'd gotten home from job hunting and sat down on my couch. I didn't remember nodding off. I don't know why I lied. There's nothing wrong with taking an occasional nap. It's not a crime. The gun was sitting in my lap.

"Too much sleep is a sign of depression. People sleep because they don't want to be awake."

"I wasn't..."

"I didn't mean to wake you."

A train went past my window. The click clack click of metal wheels on metal rails sounded like the shrieking of the dead.

"Do you live on the El tracks?" the voice asked.

I was surprised she could hear it. My phone carried more than I realized. Telephones baffle me. I've never understood how a teeny-tiny wire can carry someone's voice across thousands of miles and make it sound like that person is in the room with you. It just doesn't make sense.

"Hello?"

"Sorry," I said. "I got distracted. Who is this?"

"Is Clara there?"

"No."

"Do you know when she'll be back?"

"There is no Clara," I said. "You have a wrong number."

"Is this 856-8000?"

"Yes."

There was a pause. I wasn't sure if I was supposed to say more. I twisted the receiver cord around my finger.

"Oh my God," the voice said. "I'm so sorry. This is Clara's old number, before she moved in with Mark."

"That's okay."

"I didn't realize they reassigned numbers so fast."

I didn't say anything.

"Sorry to bother you," she said. Then she hung up.

***

The next time the phone rang, I was awake.

"Is Clara there?" It was a guy.

"This is Clara's old number," I said, "before she moved in with Mark."

"Do you know Clara?"

"Yes," I lied. "She's pretty," I added.

"I'll say. All that blonde hair. She's somethin'."

"Yes."

"Where do you know Clara from?"

"Here and there."

"Some of us are starting to get worried," he said. "We haven't seen her for a while."

"That's too bad."

"When's the last time you saw her?"

"I haven't seen her for a while, a long, long while. It seems like forever."

"I hope she's okay."

"Me, too."

"Sorry to bother you," the voice said. Then he hung up.

***

I interviewed at a cereal factory for a job working with marshmallows. I talked to a guy named James. The factory was on the outskirts of the city. I had to take the train to and from the interview.

***

I kept getting calls for Clara. Some were from her friends; some were from people that seemed to barely know her. Sometimes I pretended I knew Clara, sometimes I didn't. I looked forward to the wrong numbers. I liked talking to the people who knew her. I gathered information.

"She moved up here to be an actress," a female voice told me.

"Was she good?"

The voice laughed. "That didn't matter. It was what she wanted to do and she was going to do it no matter what."

"She was determined."

"She did some plays in high school and some people told her she was talented, so she decided to try her luck. When she got here, she didn't really do much. Some of us went to see her in a David Mamet thing at a storefront."

"A storefront?"

"One of those small theaters? They used to be retail, now they're art palaces?"

I'd seen them here and there. "I don't go to plays," I said.

"The play wasn't very good, but she was okay."

I found out that she and Mark became a quick item.

"She met him at Starbuck's that's where she worked," a man's voice said.

"That's where I met her, too," I lied. "I like coffee."

"He was a regular, stopping in every day. After a while he asked her out."

"And she said yes."

"The first time she brought Mark around to meet all of us, we weren't nuts about him. We went to this Mexican place for Margaritas. Mark was polite, but you could kind of tell he didn't want to be there. Like he didn't really care for us."

"Maybe he didn't care for the Margaritas," I said.

"Maybe," the voice agreed.

I was told about Mark and Clara moving in together.

"It was so fast," a female voice told me. "We were all a little skeptical, but it seemed to be what she wanted."

"Then it was good," I said.

"No! It wasn't! Right after she moved in with him, Mark told her she should give up her theater hobby."

"Her hobby?"

"That's what he called it. He told her that there were just too many actresses in Chicago, that no matter how talented she was she'd always get lost in the shuffle. He said he was telling her because he believed in her and didn't want to see her get hurt."

From the things the wrong numbers said to me, from talking to the people who knew Clara, I grew to know Clara, too.

***

Listening to Clara's dreams, I was reminded of my own.

Futures trading was invented in Chicago. This is what prompted me to move to the City of Big Shoulders. I wasn't crazy, I knew I wouldn't just walk into the Chicago Mercantile Exchange and be handed a million dollars. I thought I'd get a job as an office boy or in the mail room and then work my way up. I'd have my first million by the time I was forty.

The apartment I found was a single room with a kitchenette along one wall and a bathroom in the corner, no curtains and tiles instead of carpet. Elevated trains passed by right outside my window. I thought, "This place is perfect! It's so urban! True rags to riches!" It was just me, my future fortune and the sounds of the thriving metropolis.

It wasn't as perfect as I thought. I didn't become an office boy at the Merc. I didn't get a job in the mailroom at the Chicago Board of Trade. I couldn't get as much as an interview anywhere in the financial district.

All I had to hope for was working with marshmallows.

And the elevated trains never stopped.

Every time a train went past, every time I heard the screech and scream, every time my skull tore open, I felt a little bit of me leaving. My convictions climbed onto each of those trains and went to who knows where.

Honestly, can anybody trade on the future?

***

"Is Clara there?" the voice said. Another female.

"No. Sorry."

"I think something's happened to her."

"What do you mean?"

"I think something bad has happened to Clara."

The voice hung up.

My phone didn't ring for a while after that.

***

I waited.

And waited.

And waited.

I was supposed to go in for a second interview at the cereal factory, but I didn't feel up to it. I stayed home and sat and stared at the phone like a cheerleader without a prom date.

"I think something bad has happened to Clara."

What did that mean? What had happened to her? Was Clara still alive?

I slept sitting up, with the phone in my lap.

Finally, two days later, the phone rang.

"Were you asleep?" the voice said. It was female.

"No."

"They found Clara's body."

I swallowed. "Was it Mark?"

Silence.

"Did he shoot her?"

More silence.

"Are you Clara?"

The line went dead.

A train flew by my window, screaming towards its destiny.

***

I checked the papers. They found Clara in an alley. Behind a dumpster. In the eight hundred block of Chicago Avenue. According to the White Pages, she and Mark had moved to 808 Chicago.

The same block where I'd found the gun.

Clara had one bullet in her.

I looked at my pistol. Clara's calls started right after I found the weapon. Did it mean anything? Was it a coincidence? Was my gun an instrument for talking to people far away, but farther than the other side of town or even the other side of the world?

The phone rang one more time after that.

"It's all up to you," was all that was said.

***

I dressed in the same outfit I'd been wearing to job interviews, jeans and a dress shirt. I left the shirt un-tucked so I could hide the gun in my waistband.

It wasn't hard getting into the building; I waited outside until one of the tenants got home and then followed them in. I took the elevator up to the apartment.

I knocked. A man with short dark hair and glasses opened the door. He was wearing shorts and a t-shirt. I guessed he didn't plan on going outside.

"Are you Mark?" I asked.

"Yes."

"Is Clara here?"

"Do I know you?"

"No."

Something crawled across Mark's face. I couldn't tell if it was sorrow, guilt or confusion. "She's gone."

"Gone?"

"She's dead."

I looked at him for a moment and let him look at me. "I know."

The muscles in Mark's jaw tightened. "Are you a cop?"

"I'm Clara's friend," I said. I took the gun out of my waistband. "Is this yours?"

Mark's eyes widened. "Where did you find that?"

I raised the pistol. Mark started to close the door, but before he could I shot him in the face. The blast sounded like the earth exploding. In the distance, a train was going somewhere. I was surprised I could hear it.

I'd always assumed gunshots were louder than trains.

Alleyway Alvin

Tyler pointed at the roadkill rat that smeared the asphalt near the entrance to the alley. "That's what he eats," he said.

"Are you trying to scare me?" Emily asked. Her long, blonde hair kept blowing into her face.

"No," said Tyler with as much sincerity as he could muster. "Just telling you the risks of shortcuts."

It was a late Friday night. Emily had agreed to let Tyler walk her home after the Crimson Devil's football game. He was glad, he'd had a crush on her since freshman year, but she'd never seemed to notice him before. Now, they were debating their route in the crisp, autumn air.

"Alleyway Alvin shows his victims no mercy," Tyler continued. He hoped the stench of overflowing trash cans wasn't dampening the romantic mood he was trying to set.

"I've gone this way a thousand times," Emily said. "I've never run into or even heard of Alleyway Alvin."

"If people knew about him, there would be a city-wide panic; that's why he's the best kept secret in Currie Valley," Tyler said, adjusting his glasses. "He lurks in alleys, different ones on different nights. He waits for unsuspecting travelers to cut through and then he gets them."

"With a hook?"

"What?"

"Does he have a hook?" Emily asked.

"No. Why would he have a hook?"

"Don't these urban legend weirdoes usually get people with a hook?"

"He's not an urban legend," Tyler said. "He's real. He uses a…uh… claw hammer."

Emily rolled her eyes. "You're making this up as you go along."

"No! He got a junior from over in Clawson last October. He was just like us, cutting through a dark alley on a night like this..."

"Look, Tyler," Emily said, "You're a nice guy, but I think I can find my own way home."

"But... No, see... Alleyway Albert won't get people if they're holding hands."

"I thought you said his name was Alleyway Alvin?"

"It is! It's Alleyway Alvin! I'm just nervous because I don't want him to get us." Tyler summoned his courage and optimistically held out his hand for Emily to take.

Emily gave him a sad smile. "See you at school on Monday," she said. Then she turned into the alley and went on her way.

Tyler stood there stunned as he watched her walk away, her footsteps growing fainter and fainter. He wasn't quite sure where he went wrong. He was positive that his story would at least lead to some hand-holding, and probably everything up to and including second base. Females were confusing.

He shook his head and turned to go back the way they came, when a voice spoke behind him.

"You shouldn't have led with eating the splattered rat."

Tyler stopped and looked into the shadows, the hairs on the back of his neck twitching. "Excuse me?"

A man walked to the mouth of the alley. He had long, straggly hair and was dressed in jeans and a leather jacket. Behind him, steam rose from vents set in the back walls of the old, brick buildings. "You grossed her out," he said. "You should've started a little softer, roped her in."

"Okay."

"Maybe even opened with that hand-holding stuff."

"Thanks," Tyler said, starting to leave.

A hand grabbed his elbow. "Hold on a minute," the man said. From not far away, metal clanged on metal in the October breeze.

"I've got to go."

"Come in here," the man said, a smirk dancing in his eyes. "Cut down the alley. We'll talk about girls. I could tell you some stuff."

"I don't think…"

"Relax," the man said. "I'm not Alleyway Albert…"

Tyler tried to pull away. "Alvin," he corrected.

"I'm not Alleyway Alvin." His grip tightened on Tyler's elbow, pulling him into the shadows. "I'm just a guy who hangs out in alleys. And who doesn't like kids."

The only mercy Tyler saw that night, was that the man in the leather jacket didn't use a claw hammer or a hook.

Sunset Requiem

"Are you dead?" I asked my next door neighbor. We were in the hallway of our apartment building, around dinnertime.

"I don't think so. I'm just going to check the mail."

I didn't think he knew what he was talking about. I was pretty sure he'd been murdered.

He was about my age, early thirties, but in much better shape than me because he had time to work out. A lot of good it did him. Exercise didn't keep away the Grim Reaper.

I'd just fought traffic all the way home from the office. Someone in our building was cooking something with garlic; I could both smell it and feel it in the back of my throat. My neighbor looked okay on the surface, but I could tell something was different. A pallor I think it's called, or a rot, something like that.

"What did you do today?" I asked him.

"Nothing. I sat around. Worked out. Watched TV."

"Did you leave the building?"

"No."

"Did you make any phone calls?"

"No."

"Did you even get off the couch?"

"Only to get on the exercise bike."

I considered the situation. He lived alone. He didn't do anything. His body looked hard, like a statue in a cemetery. "I think you're deceased," I said.

He looked at me but didn't say anything.

"Hold on a second," I said.

I went into my apartment and dropped my coat and briefcase on the couch. I crossed over to my desk and scribbled some words onto a sheet of paper. Out my open window, I could hear traffic noise dying down. The sun had just set, the sky moving from orange to dark gray. I went into my bedroom and got my toolbox out of the closet. I grabbed what I needed; it felt heavy in my hand.

I'd lived in the building for three years. He'd been next to me all three. I knew him, but not well. He was a good neighbor. Friendly. Quiet. In a word: neighborly. It wasn't fair. I was the one working myself to death, not him. Here I was, working every day, treating my body like garbage, never catching a break. There he was, living off an inheritance, taking good care of himself, always a smile on his face. A good life! In a tiny way, I'd always been jealous of him.

When I got back out to the hallway, he was still waiting.

"Here." I handed him the sheet of paper and my finger brushed against his wrist. His skin was cold. "I wasn't sure how to spell your last name."

"What is this?"

"A death certificate."

"I'm pretty sure I'm not dead."

"I'm sorry for your loss," I said.

He started to say something, but before he could speak I cracked him in the head with my claw hammer. I'd been holding it in plain sight, but he didn't notice. Lack of vision, another sign that he was gone. The first blow put him on the floor. After five more his muscles stopped quivering.

Such a shame, he was such a lucky guy. He seemed to have it all. Yet there he was.

Murdered.

Life can be so unfair.

Mama's Drapes

Mama's soul is in them kitchen curtains.

Stackin' dishes in the sink, Mama plopped over dead. She managed to reach up and grasp the curtains as she fell.

I believe her soul went into those thin yellow pieces of cloth.

I lived with her all my life. I never married, just stayed at home. Men didn't seem to want me. Not pretty enough, I guess. Livin' with her, I knew how she was. That's why I understand about her spirit and her choice of eternal resting place.

She always loved curtains, or as she called 'em, drapes. To me a drape goes from ceiling to floor, but Mama used that word to describe any fabric hangin' in a window. She'd buy new ones whenever we could afford to, which wasn't often. "New drapes make the house look fresh," she'd say.

Now she's restin' in them.

People came over after her funeral. They saw the kitchen window and said, "You ought to fix those, Diane. Hangin' that way, you'll get bad memories." They don't get that Mama put the drapes like that, crooked and all, it's the last thing she ever did. I want to leave them that way for just a little bit longer.

It's cold now, frost on the ground in the morning. When warm weather gets here, I'll re-hang Mama's drapes. Then I'll be able to open the kitchen window and let those pieces of fabric and soul flow in the breeze.

I expect she'll like that.

A Night for Chicken Pizza

It was 10:30 after a long Saturday and Cassidy and I were hungry, so we bought a chicken wing pizza at Currie Valley Pizza Works — wing sauce, chicken and cheese. Not my preference, but it was Cassidy's favorite and I wanted him to have something he liked. Then we picked up a six-pack of Rolling Rock and I said "Let's go over by the river."

We sat on the hood of my Dodge Ram and started eating. It was a cool night, but not cold. The Mississippi flowed past. I was thinking it would be nice to have Angie with us. I assume Cassidy was thinking the same thing.

My best friend. My wife. Thinking about it, my shoulders tightened.

Cassidy was picking bits of chicken off his pizza slice and tossing them into the water. "Do you think fish like chicken?" he asked.

"I don't know," I said, trying to relax.

"Okay, then," he said, taking a bite of his pizza.

We ate for a moment or two. The pizza felt like it was boiling in my stomach. A red-tailed hawk flew overhead. We both watched it sail past, its wingspan seeming to stretch from sea to shining sea.

"There should be fireworks every night," Cassidy said, looking at the sky.

"Every night?"

"Sure! Like at the Vet's Home on the 4th, but every single night. It'd give everything a little more pizzazz."

"I don't know," I said. "Fireworks once or twice a year are special. If they were going off every night, they'd be less so."

He thought about this for a moment. "Okay, then."

We finished eating and, while Cassidy was busy collecting our trash, I got my Glock out of the glove compartment in the truck. I walked down to the riverbank and looked at the water.

"Not a bad night," I said.

"No," Cassidy agreed. "This was fun."

Without turning to look at him I said, "I know about you and Angie."

Cassidy stopped what he was doing. "You… uh…What do you… What are you talking about?"

"It happened last Thursday, right? That night I had to work late?"

Cassidy walked over and stood next to me. He looked out at the river, too – I assume because he didn't want to look at me. "I don't know what…"

"Don't lie to me."

His eyes searched the water. Was he looking for a story to tell me? A reason? An excuse? "She didn't want it to happen. I didn't want it to happen," he said. "It just happened."

"That doesn't make any sense."

"We were both drunk. It was a stupid lapse in judgement. That's all it was, just stupid."

"That's all it was?"

"That's all."

I pretended to think about that for a minute. There was tension between us that felt like the beginning of a storm.

"I'm sorry," Cassidy said. "I'm sorry it happened."

I let his apology fill the air for another second. "Okay, then," I said.

"You're not mad?"

I answered him by raising the gun to his head and pulling the trigger. At the sound of the gunshot, a couple of mourning doves launched themselves out of a nearby tree. The stench of cordite combined with the muddy smell of the river as Colin fell forward into the water with a gentle splash.

I kicked his body a few times. "Of course I'm fucking mad, you stupid piece of shit!" I shouted at him. "Did you actually fucking think I wouldn't be fucking mad!"

When I was done kicking his corpse, I leaned against the truck and let the anger drain out of me. Then I pushed Cassidy's body out into the water and watched the current carry him away.

I picked up the rest of our trash and got into my truck. I drove around for another hour or so, looking at the street signs I'd seen a million times and the stores and houses I'd seen a million and one. Listening to the classic rock station on the radio. Thinking about my former best friend. Thinking about my wife.

I'd see her next.

Maybe there should be fireworks every night. Maybe nothing's special.

Larcenous Zydeco

"I was in the Chart Room, nursing an Abita Amber, standing back by the jukebox," Justin said. "I heard these two guys sitting at the bar. They say this old fella has a cardboard box full of money. Doesn't trust banks, he's been throwing his dollars in the box his whole life."

"And he's an old guy?" Zev asked.

Justin nodded. "In his forties."

"Must be a fortune."

"And then some," Justin agreed.

The two men were sitting in Justin's car looking at the home of Sebastian Babineaux on Bayou Lafourche, twenty-five miles southwest of The Big Easy. The house was a one-story brick affair with a peaked, shingled roof and hurricane shutters on the windows. Spanish moss dripped from an ancient oak tree on the front lawn and the bayou rolled lazily along just past the old man's backyard.

"I didn't realize his house would be this close to the water," Justin said, looking at the swamp. "You think there are snakes swimming around back there?"

"Who cares!" Zev said. "We're not going in the water."

"Right. Let's just bust in and take the money. You got the gun?"

Zev took a pistol from his waistband.

"Great," Justin said. "If there's anybody in there, shoot first and ask questions later."

Zev put the gun back into his pants and the two bandits stepped out of Justin's car. They could smell the musky dampness of the bayou a few feet away. As they walked into Sebastian Babineaux's front yard, Justin wondered if the old man ever had any snakes slither into his house. He'd heard about that, snakes sneaking in through cracks in the foundation or the plumbing, and taking up residences in the walls of a home. He, personally, would never live this close to such slimy vermin.

"You okay?" Zev asked.

"Fine," Justin said.

They walked cautiously toward the house, the sounds of splashes in the water and birds screeching warnings in the air. Before they could reach the large oak in the front lawn, from around the corner of the house came a seven-foot-long alligator.

The two men stopped in their tracks.

The reptile did likewise.

Everyone looked at everyone.

"That's a big gator," Zev said.

"Not the biggest I've seen," Justin said, "but considerable."

"Where did you ever see an alligator bigger than that?"

"At the zoo."

"At the zoo doesn't count. I'm talking about in the wild."

"Oh," Justin said. "I've never seen an alligator in the wild before."

"How much you think it weighs?"

"A lot."

The alligator looked from man to man, seemingly understanding their debate on her size. The air was hot and didn't move.

"Maybe it'll go away," Justin said.

"She ain't gonna go away," said a third voice.

Justin and Zev looked toward the voice. Standing in the front door of the house was a man in his late forties wearing overalls and holding a dirty sock in his left hand.

"That's Gumdrop," said the old man. "She's somewhat of a pet, somewhat of a watchdog."

"Are you Mister Babineaux?" Justin asked.

"I am. What can I do for you two gentlemen?"

"We stopped by to… uh… Did we catch you putting on your shoes?"

Sebastian Babineaux held up the dirty sock. "Putting on my shoes?" he said. "This sock's filthy! I was taking it off. You think I walk around all day wearing dirty socks?"

"No, sir," Justin said. "I didn't mean any offense… We, uh, we came here to…"

"Let me guess, you heard I kept a giant box of money and you drove out here to relieve me of it."

Justin had to think for a moment to come up with a lie as an alternative to the truth the old man already knew. "No, sir! We were…We would never…"

"Let's just go back to the car," Zev said out of the side of his mouth.

Justin nodded and both men took a cautious step back toward their automobile. Gumdrop took a couple of energetic steps toward them. Justin and Zev halted their retreat. Gumdrop stopped and tilted her head.

"Gumdrop doesn't like suspicious movement," Sebastian Babineaux said.

"Sorry," Justin said. His muscles felt tight with fear and he could feel the tension emanating from his partner's skin. "Be cool, Zev," he said.

"I get folks coming out here all the time looking for that treasure. Do I look like the type of fool that would keep his life savings in a cardboard box in the linen closet?"

"No, sir," Justin said. "I… We wanted to ask about…"

"I'm going," Zev said and took another step toward the car. Gumdrop turned her head to follow his movement and shifted her large tail. "This is stupid," Zev said. He stopped and pulled the gun from his waistband. He pointed it at the old man in the doorway. "Call off your gator, Mr. Babineaux!"

"I wouldn't do that, son."

"I've shot people before and I'm not afraid…" Before Zev could finish, Gumdrop ran across the front lawn and grabbed him by the leg. Zev screamed and dropped the gun. Gumball's powerful jaws clamped down hard on his calf and Zev fell to the ground. The prehistoric beast dragged Zev to the bayou's edge and into the water.

It was all over in a matter of seconds.

"Guess I don't have to feed her tonight," Sebastian Babineaux said.

Justin looked around in a daze. The tree. The house. The old man in the doorway. The stench of mud and rotten vegetation and the outcries of birds. Everything was the same with one exception – Zev was gone.

Well, he'd never been that fond of his reprobate colleague anyway.

His eyes landed on Zev's fallen pistol, nestled in the Bermudagrass. Justin picked it up and pointed it at Sebastian Babineaux. "You might not have a big box of money," he said. "But since I came all the way out here, why don't we take a look at what you do have that might be worth taking?"

"I'd be careful," the old man said.

"Why? Your somewhat of a pet, somewhat of a watchdog alligator is busy at the moment."

From the back yard came charging the biggest alligator Justin had ever seen, either in the wild or at the zoo.

"Gumdrop's been having a gentleman caller drop by," Sebastian Babineaux said. "This is Lemonhead."

Justin had the wherewithal to fire off a couple of shots at the rampaging alligator, missing with each one. With molten-lava steel-edged pain, the monster lizard latched onto his foot, pulling him off-balance, and dragged him to the water's edge.

The last thought Justin had before he went under the murky depths was that he hoped there weren't any snakes.

Blue Bullet Waltz

On the way up, the Tom Waits song *Cold Cold Ground* was playing in the elevator. Not an elevator-music version of it, but the actual song. Even though I was by myself, the tight little box felt stuffy and cramped. The music made it more bearable.

When I reached the ninth floor, I stepped off and looked down the long, beige hallway for Apartment 903. It was to the left. I checked the gun in my pocket, a Browning Hi-Power Standard, then knocked on the door.

A short, round man with glasses answered.

"Hello?" he asked.

"Are you Frank Garson?"

"Yes."

"I believe I have something for you."

"Oh," he said. "Yes. Of course. Come in."

I followed Frank in. He shut the door behind me. "Can I get you something to drink," he asked.

"This isn't a social call."

"Yes. Of course. This is just… this is how you make your living. You're working."

"Trying to."

He disappeared for a minute, leaving me standing alone in his living room. His couch looked comfortable, his chairs, too. The air was just right. That was the word for his life, comfortable. Any type of edge had been left at the elevator. It all made my throat feel tight.

When he came back, he had an envelope in his hand. He handed it to me like I was a dog with a disease. "It's all there," Frank said. "You can count it if you want."

"I trust you. If it's short, I know where you live." He didn't seem to know whether I was making a joke or a threat.

I took the Browning out of my pocket and showed it to him. "Do you know how to use one of these?"

"Is it much different than what I see in movies?"

"Pretty much the same, just louder. Don't tilt it to try to look cool."

He smiled. "I don't try to look cool."

I handed him the gun. He weighed it in his hand. The silence stretched between us. He must have felt like he had to say something. "I… I need it for protection…" His eyes wouldn't meet mine. "I doubt… I hope I'll never even use it."

Sure. That's why he needed an untraceable weapon. "You need anything else?" I asked.

"No. Thank you! You've been very helpful."

He showed me out then locked his door behind me. Comfortably safe.

While I waited for the elevator, I wondered if I'd read a newspaper article about a jealous husband shooting his wife's lover, or a quiet employee shooting up his office, or a down-on-his-luck loser robbing a bank.

I didn't care one way or the other.

On the way down, there was more Tom Waits — *Trouble's Braids*. Whoever the Building Manager was, they had taste.

The elevator was stuffy and cramped, but it felt more honest than comfort.

Words Fall Like Nothing

"Kiss me before you go," Janis said.

I grabbed her and forced my lips onto hers.

"Christ! You need to relax, baby," she said. "Loosen up. Kissing you is like kissing a brick wall."

I got out of the car. She leaned across the seat as I closed the door. "Get out of there as fast as you can. Don't dawdle! And if it looks like it's going bad, wave at me so I can figure out our next move."

I nodded. I knew what 'our' next move would be, Janis leaving and me dealing with the aftermath.

I walked into the Currie Valley Savings and Loan. The Tom Jones version of Prince's *Kiss* played as I walked past plastic plants, free coffee and the 'Please Wait Here For Next Available Teller' sign. No one else was around, just me, a guard who had probably been on the job for the last thirty years and a pretty, middle-aged teller named Marie.

"How can I help you today," Marie asked.

I pulled the gun out of my waistband and pushed an empty duffel bag towards her. Marie knew what I wanted.

"You can have it all," she said. "Just don't hurt anybody."

Marie started filling up the bag with money. I was sweating, the air in the Savings and Loan hadn't been adjusted for the warm, spring weather. While I watched Marie, I thought about Janis.

This was her idea. Grab some quick cash and then get out of town. Somewhere warm, somewhere exotic, somewhere romantic. Romance – it was the opposite of what Janis and I had.

We'd met at Puzzles Pub, down by the river. A Wednesday – 'All You Can Eat Spaghetti Night.' I was alone, she was my waitress. Blonde hair, stout but supple lips and curves. We went back to my place. She moved in a week later and quit her job the week after that. Now if we went to Puzzles, she got drunk and caused a scene, talking about how she climbed out of that Hell-hole.

Crawled out of one Hell-hole to create a new one – my life.

Janis lived like a pig; dishes piled in the sink, clothes thrown all over the apartment, wet towels slopped on the bathroom floor. She slept most of the day and stayed out most of the night. And if Janis didn't have anything rotten to say, she didn't say anything at all:

"Why don't you clean this dump?"

"Try not to embarrass me when we go out tonight."

And my favorite, "Is that it?" after sex.

Everything we talked about, every discussion we had turned into an argument, usually going on for hours and usually ending with Janis telling me I was a retard.

"Take it," Marie said, bringing me back to where I was and what I was going. "Take the money and please don't hurt anyone." The duffel bag was bulging.

I nodded politely, took my bag full of cash and headed for the door. The security guard was standing in front of it with his gun drawn.

"Folks leaving with a duffel bag in one hand and a gun in the other is a red flag," he said.

I stopped. His gun was aimed right at me, mine was down at my side. No way he could miss.

Outside, through the glass doors, I could see Janis sitting in the car, drumming her fingers on the steering wheel. As I watched, she got an annoyed look on her face and started honking the horn.

"Is that your ride?" the guard asked.

I nodded.

"Sounds a little impatient."

I looked out at Janis again. Anything seemed better than getting back in that car with her. I looked back at the guard.

"Don't do anything stupid, son," he said, seeing something in my eyes. "This is the end. You can't get past me."

I lifted my gun. The guard was ready. He fired. I smiled as I fell.

As the hole in my chest leaked onto the cold marble floor, I brought my hand to my mouth, turned my head and blew Janet a goodbye kiss.

It was better than talking things to death.

In Lieu of Crimson Roses

Kevin's fist flattened my nose against my face, the cartilage sprawling across my cheekbones, blood surging over my mouth and lips, my eyes filling with water. Bells went off inside my brain. The pain was like discordant music played on shards of glass.

Fifteen minutes later, I was at her door.

Lauren's voice came through the intercom like the song of an angel drifting down from Heaven. "Hello?"

"It's Jake. From work."

"What do you want?"

"Can I come up?"

"What do you want?"

I let the pain creep into my voice. I'd rehearsed this part on the way over. "I got beat up."

The buzzer sounded and I let myself in.

Lauren and I both worked at Hot Stan's, the best hot pretzel purveyor in the Currie Valley Mall. You probably think that Hot Stan's is the only hot pretzel purveyor in the Currie Valley Mall, but you're wrong. The mall also has Mother May's Pretzels and the sports bar, Diamond Doug's, has hot pretzels as an appetizer. As far as hot pretzels go, Mother May and Diamond Doug are both garage bands and Hot Stan's is Van Halen.

Lauren had worked at Hot Stan's for about six months. She had dark hair streaked with gold, a relaxed laugh and she made the orange Hot Stan's aprons we had to wear look sexy. Aside from her habit of losing her patience with some of our more dim-witted customers, I thought she was perfect.

In the eleven years I'd been with the company, I'd asked out several of the women that got hired. Each time I brought in a single red rose and made my pitch. They all said no.

Lauren was standing in her open doorway when I got to the top of the stairs, wearing jeans and a grey Knights of Columbus t-shirt. Her hair was down and I realized I'd never seen her out of her hairnet. Her eyes inflated when she saw me. I knew why. My right eye was puffed shut. My nose was destroyed. Various gashes, scratches, slashes and cuts criss-crossed my face.

"What happened?"

I'd rehearsed this part, too. "I was taking my trash out," I said. "This guy jumped me in the alley behind my building."

"Why?"

"I don't know. Maybe he wanted money. I don't know. He ran off."

She ushered me inside, sat me down on her couch and then went to her bathroom. She had a nice place, small but she used the space well. There were Polaroids on the walls, pictures of Lauren in bars and at parties, canoeing on the river, lying on a beach next to an ocean.

When she came back, she carried Q-tips, towels, hydrogen peroxide and Band-Aids. She pulled up a chair in front of me and started wiping away some of the blood. Her eyes looked sympathetic and a little disgusted. "Does it hurt?"

"Only when I laugh," I said, trying to be as smooth as the pain would let me.

"Why did you come here?" she asked as she worked.

I looked at her for a moment. I hadn't rehearsed this part. The symphony of agony I felt in my head made it hard to think. "I thought I might…" I couldn't come up with anything. "I think he wanted my wallet."

She stopped working on my face. "But why did you come here?"

I gave myself another moment. "This was the only place I could think of."

She started to work again.

"I think your nose is broken."

"Probably. He's pretty strong."

"He? Who's he?"

"I mean, he hit me pretty hard. He must be strong."

"Did you know the person that did this to you?"

My throat tightened. I could smell Lauren's hair, like flowers and oranges.

"We could go get a pizza," I said.

Lauren stopped again. "What's going on here?"

"Or Chinese."

Lauren stood up from her chair. "I think you should leave," she said, turning to head for the door.

"I just…"

Lauren paused and looked at me. "You just what?"

I stood. It felt like her eyes were burning holes in my face. "I read somewhere that the best way to jump-start a relationship is with the help of a disastrous catalyst. Something bad happens and it gives two people a reason to need each other. Like the loss of a job, or a natural disaster or something as simple as a mugging. Any of these can make two people say 'We'll get through this together.'"

"You came here to…" She shook her head. "Who did this to you?"

"Kevin."

"That guy you hang out with?"

"He's my best friend." I tried a quirky smile. "A best friend is the best choice if you want the best beating."

She started walking away again.

My hand reached out to touch her shoulder. "Can't we get through this together?"

The moment my fingers made contact, Lauren twisted back toward me, her arm moving like a fast and angry python. Her fist flattened my nose against my face, the cartilage sprawling across my cheekbones, blood surging over my mouth and lips. My eyes filled with tears.

"You should've just asked me out, Jake," Lauren said. "I probably would've said yes."

Devotion and the Autumn Chill

"I dreamt of you last night," Lacey said. She was lying in bed, her long brown hair splayed over her pillow.

"Is that a fact?" Kyle was just back from taking a shower, his black hair damp, his skin still flush from the hot water. "That's good, right? Means I'm your true love."

They were in the small town of Spencer to help celebrate the West Virginia Black Walnut Festival. It was nearing the middle of October and the leaves on the mountain trees were turning from green to gold.

They usually stayed in cheap hotels one or two towns away from the festivals they hit. This time, at Lacey's insistence for romance, they stayed at the Bugle Family Bed and Breakfast. When they were checking in, Kyle told Mrs. Bugle it was their honeymoon. The lie was partly a cover story and partly an insult to Lacey. He'd made it very clear to her, both in conversation and in action, that he never planned to marry her.

Unaware of the untruth, Mrs. Bugle's eyes lit up. "I have a special room just for newlyweds."

"Is that a fact," Kyle said.

"The bed has a hand-made Devotion Quilt."

"What's that?" Lacey asked.

"The first time you sleep under a Devotion Quilt, you dream about love."

Lacey noticed Kyle roll his eyes.

"You see true love in its true light," Mrs. Bugle said.

Lacey wasn't much for arts and crafts. She didn't foresee an instance in her life where she would need to know how to knit or crochet. She'd never been inspired to make a pot with just her hands and the clay of the earth. She couldn't tell the difference between a quilt, a blanket and a comforter. Lacey wasn't much for arts and crafts, but she and Kyle drove all over the Appalachia region.

They'd been to the Jackson County Apple Festival, the Cave Run Storytelling Festival and the Shaker Woods Folk Festival. They'd visited three or four Heritage Days.

Once, when money was particularly low, they'd even stopped at a company picnic at the Beckley Exhibition Coal Mine. But their main bread and butter came from straight-up arts and crafts events. That was where people had the most to sell, so that was where people had the most money.

Today was the first day of the Black Walnut extravaganza.

Lacey shifted under the bed covers. "It wasn't a nice dream," she said, reaching her hand up toward the headboard.

"Is that a fact?" Kyle didn't even look at her as he finished buttoning up his shirt.

"You were with another woman."

Kyle tucked in his shirt. "It was just a dream." The smell of fresh baked cinnamon rolls drifted into their room from downstairs.

They'd been together for a little over two years. It took Kyle almost seven months to convince Lacey to join him in his enterprise. He'd made it sound like they'd be folk heroes. He said the festivals had presidents and committees and all sorts of other people that made money on the sweat of the vendors and performers. These organizers would claim that the event was 'to preserve the remnants of Appalachia traditional life and culture,' but that wasn't the case. Kyle told her that somebody was always turning an ill-gotten profit.

Kyle also mesmerized Lacey with whispers about dreams come true and commitment and true love.

They would get into town at the beginning of the festival and just observe. In addition to Kyle's talent for picking pockets, they would figure out who the VIPs were and, with a little snooping, find out what financial institution the festival committee used. Since the bank was closed on Sunday, both Saturday's and Sunday's profits would be deposited Monday morning. Kyle and Lacey would wait outside the bank on Monday until they saw one of the faces from the fair. The bigwigs usually made it easy by carrying the money in something visible like a canvas bag or a cashbox. Then Kyle pulled the gun and Lacey drove the getaway car.

Today was their first day of work. If previous festivals were any indication, this work would include Lacey sitting alone in the cooling weather and scrutinizing every aspect of the operation while Kyle flirted with the Miss Black Walnut contestants.

Kyle fastened his belt.

"You were with another woman," Lacey said again. The bed sheets felt cool against her skin.

Kyle didn't say anything. Outside the window a cardinal sang.

From underneath Kyle's pillow, Lacey drew his pistol and aimed it at him.

Now she had his attention. "Honey," Kyle said. "You know you don't like that thing."

"True love in its true light."

"That's just a bunch of old wives' superstition."

Lacey thought about becoming an old wife and about betrayal and about folk heroes. She thought about traditional life. She thought about dreams come true and devotion and true love. "Superstition?" she asked him.

"It was just a dream," Kyle gave her a smile, the cornerstone of his charm.

Lacey smiled back. "Is that a fact?" she said. Then she pulled the trigger.

They never even made it to the festival.

Sparrows & Crows

A knife given as a present cuts the friendship, or so they say. Tyrone didn't actually give me his knife as a gift, he loaned it to me and I just never gave it back, but it still had the same effect.

"Bored?"

"Yeah."

"Let's go do something."

We had the same phone conversation every night. Sometimes I had the opening lines, sometimes he did, but it always led to one of us picking the other up and then driving around until it was time to go home.

That was our lives, a whole lot of nothing. Boredom. Monotony. A complete absence of anything inspiring or worthy of note, every day our lives and souls growing a little bit more vacant.

He picked me up fifteen minutes after the call. Tyrone was a tall guy, six foot two, and he always looked like he was folded into his mid-size car.

"Where's Diana?" I asked as I got in the car.

"Out with some friends."

Over the years, we'd both had girlfriends. Tyrone went through them faster than I did thanks to his problem with being faithful. Some of Tyrone's companions I liked, some I didn't, and it was the same for him with the women I dated. We never let our conquests come between us.

His latest was Diana, a five-foot three-inch waitress at the IHOP on Halsted. It was amusing seeing them together, one really tall, one really short. They looked like they could be a comedy team. When he first introduced me to her, she greeted me by saying, "What's your goal?"

I was at a loss. "My goal?"

"Yeah. You know. What's your goal in life?"

I didn't like that question, both because I thought it was a little abrupt, having just met her, and also because I didn't have a goal.

"I don't know," I said. "What's yours?"

"To live," she said.

She grew on me a little over time, but not much. I figured I'd better get used to her being around, since Tyrone had confided in me that she was 'The One'.

"What do you want to do?" I asked him as he pulled away from the curb.

"There's nothing to do."

"I know."

He paused and turned to face me. His response was an unexpected cliché, an out-of-the-blue sitcom joke. "Let's kill a drifter and get rid of the body."

I looked at him.

"You heard me," he said. "You up for it?"

"You're serious?"

"Why not? Killing some bum, who would care?"

It's funny how inactivity makes almost any idea seem like a good one.

I know the difference between right and wrong, between good and evil, between amusement and cruelty, but I was bored. Every day and every night it was the same thing. Work. Hang out. Sleep. Work. Hang out. Sleep. Work. Hang out. Sleep. This, the endless song of the world-weary, combined with Tyrone's question into a spur of the moment philosophy.

Why not? If being alive was this tedious, maybe life had no meaning. If life was this uninteresting, this boring, this dull, then maybe life wasn't that valuable. For something to have value, after all, it has to be rare. And life is the one thing on the planet that every living person has. Rather than being valuable, life was the most common, lackluster commodity there could be.

"So, are you up for it?" Tyrone asked again.

"Why not," I said.

***

We met in the seventh grade. We were both brand new thirteen-year-old teenagers. Tyrone's older brother, Teddy, had just died of Leukemia. Tyrone was pretty messed up about it. One minute he'd be crying quietly to himself, the next screaming at the world. I don't think he ever got over it. When we met, I became the brother he lost and he became the brother I never had. He was my roommate in college and after graduation we moved to Chicago together. We took separate apartments; we were friends, but we'd had enough of living with each other.

Usually, when we drove around, we circled, like we were looking for parking, but with a wider radius and lower expectations. This night, after we picked up some supplies at the Osco drugstore near Addison, we stuck to our usual route: south on Broadway, west on Belmont, north on Ashland, east on Wilson. We were circling again, but this time as predators.

We found her on Belmont, just off of Clark. Wrigley Field was only a couple blocks away. She had filthy clothes and matted hair and was bothering people with the customary street line: "Can you spare any change?" When her potential benefactors didn't respond, she mumbled things at them as they continued down the street.

"Hey," I called out the window.

She ignored me. She was probably used to people yelling insults at her as they drove by.

"Hello," I tried again.

Nothing.

"You hungry?"

This got her attention.

"Yeah."

"Get in."

She looked at Tyrone's car and had a dialogue with herself under her breath.

"Come on," I said. "We're not going to hurt you. We're just trying to do a good deed."

"You sure?" she asked.

"We're sure." Tyrone smiled as he said it.

She talked to herself again, I suppose to convince herself that we were okay, and then climbed into the back seat. Tyrone turned north.

"What's your name?" Tyrone asked.

"Jamie."

"I'm Tyrone. This is Josh. Burger King alright?"

"Fine."

"What's your story?" I asked. I wasn't sure if I really wanted to know.

She didn't answer; she just watched the storefronts pass as we drove by.

"How did you end up on the street?" I tried again.

"I was married," Jamie said, still looking out the window. "Had a good job, too. They let me go because they were cutting back, whatever that means. After that, Gary left."

"Gary?"

"I don't blame him, I got real depressed. I was a receptionist with a doctor's office for fifteen years! After they let me go, I woke up every day feeling awful. I didn't feel like finding another job and didn't feel like making my marriage work. I don't blame Gary for leaving, but I sure do miss him. He's been gone ten years."

"We can't give you any money," Tyrone said, "but we can get you something to eat. And we can drive you to a homeless shelter."

She didn't respond. She had rejoined the conversation that only she could hear.

We stopped at a Burger King on Irving Park and I went inside while Tyrone stayed in the car with Jamie. I bought her a whopper with cheese and extra onions. I took the food into the men's room and locked the door.

From out of my pocket I took a bottle of sleeping pills. I opened the sandwich and crumbled the pills onto the meat, the extra onions covering their taste. On my way back out, I caught a glimpse of myself in the mirror. It didn't look like me. I looked away and got out of there before I had to think about who or what had been staring back from the glass.

"This is really nice," Jamie said as I handed her the food. She was asleep five minutes after we left the parking lot.

***

There were whitecaps on the lake. Lake Michigan is beautiful, and it's even more striking when it's angry. We were at a beach near Montrose Harbor. It was cold, the wind cutting off the water. We'd driven around for several hours with Jamie passed out in the back, waiting for the city to go to sleep, and now it was well into the middle of the night.

"See anybody?" Tyrone asked as soon as we'd stepped out of the car.

I looked around. There were birds hopping around nearby in the sand. It seemed strange, seeing birds after dark.

"Just us and the sparrows and crows."

"That's a good name for a band," Tyrone said. "Sparrows and Crows."

I smiled and nodded my head a little. I didn't feel good.

Tyrone dragged Jamie's unconscious body out of the backseat and down to the water. Jamie didn't stir. At first I was a concerned that we'd used too many sleeping pills and killed her. Isn't that stupid, considering what we planned to do? Then I saw Jamie's chest rising and falling and I was able to breathe again.

"Are you sure we want to do this?" I asked him.

"Look at her. She's alive. There's nothing wrong with her. She's not blind; she's not missing an arm. Why is she homeless? She's a living, breathing person that has the chance to do anything, but she's wasting it. She's wasting her life."

"That doesn't mean we should kill her."

"We'll be doing her a favor," he said.

He pulled Jamie into the tide and laid her on her back in ankle deep water. The cold spray made her eyes twitch. I followed. Tiny waves washed over my feet while Tyrone pulled Jamie to her knees. The cold water must have penetrated the fog that enveloped Jamie. Her eyes cracked open and her mouth started to twitch with questions she was too groggy to ask. Her breath smelled like onions.

"Hold on," I said.

Tyrone ignored me. He took a hunting knife out of his pocket. It had a three-inch blade that folded into a white bone handle. When I saw it, I felt a burn crawl from the back of my throat down to the pit of my stomach. Tyrone smiled. It wasn't the world's greatest knife, but I knew it meant a lot to him. It had belonged to Teddy.

"Hold on a minute." I said it before he could open the blade.

"What?"

"You're sure?"

He nodded. "This is just between us."

I looked at my feet in the water. I couldn't feel them.

"Just between us," Tyrone said again.

I moved around behind Jamie and held her in place. "Just between us," I agreed. "And the birds."

Tyrone unfolded the knife blade and held it to Jamie's throat.

The wind stopped blowing, like it was waiting for Tyrone to start.

I tried to say something, but couldn't. I wanted to pull Jamie away from the knife, but instead I just looked back towards shore.

I heard a sharp intake of breath that could have been from either of them and then felt Jamie slip out of my hands with a splash. When I looked back, Jamie was flopping on her back in the water. She didn't shriek or yell or cry. I don't know if she couldn't, or just didn't. I wanted to, I wanted to scream, but something held me back.

I tasted salt-water and realized I was crying.

Jamie's body trembled, her hands clenched and her eyes frantically searched the sky for some kind of help. After what seemed like hours, she flipped over onto her stomach, her face reaching through the water to the sandy bottom. Lake water filled Jamie's mouth. She drowned in the ankle-deep surf.

My heart was hammering adrenaline through my system. I wanted to throw up. When I looked at Tyrone, his face was white and sweat shone on his forehead. He looked like he was shocked by what he had seen, by what he had done.

"Let's go," I said.

"Just between us."

I grabbed his arm and dragged him toward the car.

"Let's go."

***

We went on with our lives. That seems astounding now, but it's what we did.

After we left the beach, Tyrone dropped me off and I took a scalding shower that lasted for over an hour. I couldn't seem to get my feet warm. Then I went to bed.

The next morning I got up and went to work like everything was normal. I stumbled my way through my job, thinking about how Jamie didn't scream, about how none of us had screamed.

Tyrone and I called each other throughout the day, asking if the cops had shown up. That night, we didn't go out driving. We had enough to keep us occupied. We bought the Sun Times and the Tribune and watched the local news. Our crime didn't go unmentioned, but it wasn't at the top of anybody's list of priorities.

The press never mentioned it again after that first day.

We hung out and went to work and lived our lives. The cops never knocked on either of our doors. We went back to our humdrum routines. Jamie really was our little secret, just between us and the sparrows and the crows.

***

Three months later, our secret shifted.

We had picked up Diana from work and were headed to Tyrone's place to watch a movie. We were parked at the

7-Eleven on Roscoe Street, right in the heart of Boys Town. Tyrone was inside buying soda and Diana and I were sitting in the car.

"Have your ears been burning?" Diana asked from the backseat. She had a twinkle in her eye.

"Why?"

"We were talking about you."

One of the things I didn't like about Diana was that she couldn't just say what was on her mind, every conversation had to be a guessing game.

"What did the two of you say?"

"I know what you guys did."

Ice slithered through my shoes. "Some old college thing?" I asked, knowing it wasn't likely.

"No. You know what I mean."

"The beach?"

She nodded. "Don't worry, Tyrone means the world to me. He's just as guilty as you are."

"You won't tell anybody?"

"Of course not," she said. "This is just between us."

***

Six weeks after that, Tyrone and Diana broke up.

"What happened?" I asked.

"I was at Schuba's. I met this girl. We started talking…"

"You bought her drinks and she bought you drinks and you went home together. It's the same thing that always happens."

"No, it wasn't the same thing! Diana meant more than that!"

If she was more than that, I wanted to say, why did you cheat on her?

He ranted and raved for a while. He was mad at her, mad at himself, mad at the girl in the bar, mad at me, pretty much mad at everyone. He wouldn't let his eyes meet mine. One minute he said he loved Diana, the next that he hated her. He told me that one afternoon he went into a jewelry store in Water Tower Place and looked at diamond rings. He didn't try to buy anything, he didn't even talk to the clerk, he just looked. He said that the memory of that afternoon, the memory of being surrounded by diamonds, made him feel ashamed.

After he calmed down, he added one more thought. "She's going to tell."

I looked at him.

"She's really pissed at me. She threatened to go to the cops."

"The cops?"

"That's what she said."

"Why did you have to tell her?" I asked, trying to keep my voice steady.

"I couldn't help it."

"You couldn't help it? It was supposed to be a secret, but you had to tell her because you couldn't help it?"

"Sorry."

"That makes it all better. We're screwed, but you're sorry. Now everything's fine."

"I thought I'd be with her forever."

I didn't have anything left to say.

He looked at me. Our eyes made contact. "We have to take care of her."

"What do you mean?"

"We can't let her go to the cops."

"What do you mean?" I repeated.

"We have no choice."

***

We waited.

We parked in an alley next to Diana's apartment building. Tyrone said she usually got home from work around eleven. We got there at ten forty-five, got out of the car and waited. There were people here and there on the street.

She walked past at five till. Tyrone rushed out of the alley, put his hand over her mouth and dragged her back to where we'd parked. I opened the trunk. Tyrone threw her in and I closed the lid. Then we drove away. Nobody on the street yelled, nobody pointed at us, nobody did anything. I couldn't tell if they just didn't see us or just didn't care. I was beginning to believe you could get away with anything in the Windy City.

***

We took her to an abandoned storefront on Buckingham. An actor friend once told me that it was a place where small theater groups would go to rehearse. The lock on the back entrance didn't work, so they would let themselves in when they didn't have the money to rent rehearsal space. There was no electricity, but there was a little light from a streetlamp shining through an alley window. I didn't mind the darkness. I didn't really want to see what we were doing.

Diana was duct-taped to a chair. We'd been there ten minutes, nobody saying much. Diana was upset, Tyrone was upset, I was upset. I wasn't sure how we were supposed to handle this.

Tyrone stepped behind Diana's chair and took his brother's knife out of his pocket. He stood there and looked down at her. After a moment, he stepped away and looked at me. "You have to do it," he said.

"No," I said.

"I can't."

"What makes you think it'll be any easier for me?"

"I thought you were 'The One'," he said to Diana. He looked like he was going to start crying.

I walked over to him. "Let's go," I said.

"This is as much your problem as it is mine."

He was right. I didn't want to do to jail.

"Give it to me."

He pressed the knife into my hand. "Just between us."

"Sure," I said. "I'll call you when it's done."

Tyrone took one last look at Diana. "We have no choice," he said, more to himself than to either of us. Then he left.

I held the knife in my hand, felt the weight of it. I looked around the shabby room. Apparently, the theater groups didn't keep their secret clean. In the dim light, I could see garbage in the corners, old newspapers, beer bottles and fast-food bags. The air smelled of stale onions.

"Why did you do it?" Diana asked.

"I don't know."

"Come on."

"It seemed like the thing to do at the time."

"You were just bored?"

A chill crawled across the souls of my feet. I nodded. One of the newspapers in the corner shifted in a breeze that wasn't there. I felt eyes watching me, even though I knew we were alone.

I'd wasted enough time. I stepped behind the chair and unfolded Tyrone's blade. I knew that didn't change the weight of the knife, but it felt heavier.

"Sorry," I said.

I put the knife blade against Diana's throat. Tyrone was my best friend. I'd do anything for him and he'd do anything for me.

I couldn't move my hand.

I kept hearing the newspapers shifting, fluttering, trembling. They sounded like the flapping of a bird's wings.

I pushed the steel against Diana's skin, but my hand would only let it press so far. The flapping grew louder, much too loud to be a newspaper caught in the wind. I shook my head, trying to escape the sound.

Diana started sobbing. She took huge, wracking breaths that, when exhaled, smelled of stagnant water and onions. My feet felt frozen, like they were cold enough to crack.

My arm flexed.

Diana closed her eyes.

I listened to the birds, to the music of their wings.

I moved the blade over the duct tape that held Diana in place. I cut her free from the chair.

The flapping stopped.

"Get out of here," I said.

She looked at me, her eyes red, her face wet.

"Go on!"

She stood and walked out of the building.

I folded the knife and stuck it in my pocket. I never gave it back to Tyrone.

***

After that, one thing led to another, which led to another. Diana made good on the threat she made to punctuate her and Tyrone's breakup. Police came to my door as well as Tyrone's, there was a trial and now I'm sitting in a detention cell in the Cook County Department of Corrections, waiting to be shipped out to Joliet.

Our trial was downtown. It's funny, I always tried to avoid going downtown; too many shoppers and tourists. But, there's a lot Tyrone and I could've checked out. Navy Pier. The Sears Tower. Sightseeing tours.

At least it would have been something to do.

Long Black Gloves

She wore long black gloves, satin accessories that came up past her elbows, smooth and glossy to the touch. Refined. Exotic. Distinct.

I met her in the L & L Tavern on Clark Street, a dark, smoky place with Formica tables, wooden chairs, cheap drinks and a quiet but clear sense of despair. She was sitting at the bar.

I sat down on the stool next to her. She gave me a dry smile. "Buy me a drink?" she asked.

She seemed like she was already halfway there. "Of course," I said.

We drank, Jameson for her and Johnnie Walker Black for me. Neil Young's *Unknown Legend* played on the jukebox. After a couple of rounds, she asked, "Do you like my gloves?"

"Sure," I said. "I love your gloves."

"Fancy, aren't they?"

"Elegant," I said. "What's the occasion? Are you going to the opera? Or a high society ball? Or a party at an embassy?"

"I just like wearing long, black gloves."

"That's fair," I said.

"You like the way they rest on my skin? If we go somewhere, you can take them off. You can slide them down my arms, past my wrists, over my hands. Do it slow, like a ritual – methodical, leisurely, deliberate."

"How much would something like that cost?" I asked.

"I'm not a hooker. I just feel like being with somebody."

"Lonely?"

"Who isn't?" she said.

I took her home. We fumbled around on each other. Her satin hands added an interesting element to our activities. After we finished, she told me a story about a boy and a waterfront and a mugging gone bad. The boy in the story liked long, black gloves. Then, in the night as I slept, she showed herself out.

The next evening I went back to L & L. My paramour was in the same spot at the bar, gloves and all.

I sat next to her. "Did you spend it all?" I asked.

"Hi," she said.

"Did you spend my twelve dollars?"

"I did," she said. Her satin-tipped finger made small circles on the bar. "I did spend your twelve dollars. Cab fare."

"My fortune."

"Sorry. It's all gone."

"Thanks for leaving the wallet. And the credit cards."

"What would I do with your credit cards?" She took her smooth, silky hand and placed it on top of mine on the bar. It felt like a cool breeze from far away. "Thanks," she said.

"Buy you a drink?" I asked.

"Of course."

Our drinks came. We sat in silence for a moment while we appreciated them.

"Did it help?" I asked. "Last night. Did it help any?"

"Not really," she said. "Maybe a little, but not enough." She sipped her whiskey. "Still think I'm fancy?" she asked.

"Elegant," I told her.

At a table near the back, a woman laughed. "You didn't make me an omelet," she cackled. "You never made me an omelet." Her laughter sounded like glass breaking.

Breaking

I used to avoid downtown Chicago in the summer and during the Christmas shopping season. That's when the sidewalks are most crowded with tourists. I don't feel much need to be around tourists. Now I have no choice. Downtown is where I work, where I make minimum wage to barely get by.

I see them every day, waiting for me as I step off the bus. There are three of them, wearing bright t-shirts and colorful rags tied on their heads. They set up a large piece of cardboard in the middle of the sidewalk. They spin on their backs, their knees, on their heads. They move like robots. One of them even moonwalks. I thought break-dancing died in the eighties, right after *Breakin' 2: Electric Boogaloo.*

They're here every morning, every afternoon, every night. Begging for money from strangers. I've watched them, waiting.

Today is my day off, but I've come downtown anyway. And I've come prepared. Sunglasses. Hat. A plastic bag from Skyline Souvenirs. I look like a visitor from out of town.

They're supposed to have street performing licenses, these inner-city Baryshnikovs. They don't care. Just like the ice cream trucks that park in front of the Tribune Building and accept a twenty-five-dollar ticket to sell three-hundred dollars' worth of good humor. The city can't hurt them enough to make them stop.

When the cop arrives, he looks like something unnatural. He rides a Segway, standing seven feet tall on the moving platform. He has sunglasses instead of eyes. His body doesn't move, the machine does all the work with its rolling wheels.

They run in three separate directions. I follow the one that takes the collection bucket.

On the surface Chicago is allure, a gleaming Windy City, the most magnificent of Magnificent Miles. Underground it's noise and dumpsters and exhaust-spewing deliveries. Dark and blunt. Beneath the surface is the side of the city the sightseers fear.

He stops once he gets to the lower level. I'm right behind him. Inside my plastic bag is a souvenir miniature baseball bat, the size of a policeman's baton. As I bring it down on the dancer's head, I wonder if he's a Cubs fan or a Sox fan.

In the bucket is $118.37, more than twice what I make in a day. Money from tourists. I look at the kid lying on the ground. I don't feel bad. After all, I'm the one who works. All he does is spin around.

Like Sapphires in the Sea

Look down there. Sunlight glitters on the green water and makes it look like liquid emeralds. Even though I see it every day, I've never seen the river look as lucid as it does now.

I play the drums for a living, even though I don't know how. I also don't have any drums, just these upside-down plastic buckets. My drumsticks, though, these are real.

I perform in Chicago, The Loopy Second City of Windy Big Shoulders. I sit here on my sidewalk on my bridge over my river and play my drums. I give myself a morning shift (when people are walking to work) and an evening shift (when people are walking away from work). People look at me and I do my best not to get worried. Some of them give me money. I make anywhere from fifty to three hundred bucks a day. It's winter now. In the winter people give me more.

It's a living. But, sitting here, smelling garbage and bus exhaust…well, I'm glad this is my last day.

Right over there is the Jewelers Building. It's the brownish-cream colored one, with the turrets at each corner of the roof and the tower in the center. Beautiful, isn't it? At one time, most of the jewelers in Chicago had their offices in that building, hence the name. It looks like an old monastery.

There's a lot of traffic on the street. In the summer, there's a lot of traffic on the river, too. Boats pass by down there all day long, different colors, shapes and sizes. I take a few moments after each shift to watch them. No boats today; it's too cold. When the wind blows off Lake Michigan like a knife that nobody's cared about for a long time, no one wants to go near the water.

I used to have a life. Another town, another place. I saw something I shouldn't have. I was walking. I glanced down an alley and saw a bad thing. The person doing it was someone I recognized from the news. He held a metal blade that glittered in the neon light. A body fell to the pavement. I kept walking, but I guess the man I recognized saw me, too. That's why they killed Jade. They wanted to prove a point and they used her. Then I ran. They might still be after me. I ended up here, playing the drums to the distant sounds of jackhammer construction. I play and stare at the tall buildings. Some days they make me feel small.

They say Al Capone had a speakeasy on the top floor of the Jewelers Building. I don't know if it's true, but it's what people want to hear. There are so many myths about gangsters that they become caricatures, overblown characters riddled with clichés. It's easy to forget that they're real. They exist. They're out there in the world, doing bad things.

Jade and I met at the Moonstone, a blues bar in my old town that nobody seemed to know about. The darkness inside was almost always empty. I started seeing Jade there every now and then. We met listening to cover versions of Barkin' Bill, Robert Johnson and Little Walter. Our romance was scored by the musical poetry of heartache.

That's why I ran to Chicago. Because I like the blues.

When I found her, in our apartment, in our bed, her nightgown had turned as red as rubies. A break-in, while I was out. It could have been just a random robbery, but I knew it wasn't. Only one thing was missing. I don't know why they didn't wait, they could've taken me when I got home, but they didn't. They let me live. With my memories.

I came to Chicago. They might still be out there, looking. I picked up a few different jobs: coffee house, office temp, waiter. I'd be at work and I'd see someone looking at me and I'd think I'd been found. Because of that, jobs came and went. So I went into self-employment: I started playing the drums. Rather than hide with my fear, I decided to put myself in plain sight.

Did you know that in the Jewelers Building there used to be an elevator big enough to carry a car? Jewelers would load up their automobiles with diamonds and garnets and pearls, drive onto the elevator, go up to their floor and then drive off directly into their vaults. It was supposed to be the safest building in the city. This was before they knew about Al Capone's tavern. All of that safety was just an illusion.

It was a nice experiment, but hiding out in the open doesn't work. I still spend every day afraid. And remorseful. And alone. They might still be after me, they might not. There's no real way I can know. I'm tired of wondering. Either way, today is my last day.

A lot of people think all sapphires are blue, but actually they can come in several colors. I opened a checking account once upon a time and the bank gave me a sapphire for opening the account. It was a purple, flawed thing, probably worth nothing. I had it put in a setting and bought a chain to hang it from. It was the first gift I ever gave her. They didn't steal anything from our apartment, except Jade's flawed necklace. It's gone forever.

It's time. Time to put down my sticks. Time to stop playing. Time for forever.

Look down there. Cold. Green. Final. I can't swim, not that the frigid water would give me much of a chance. It'll be over before I know it.

Time to drown in emeralds.

The Thug and the
Three-Handed Lady

"Do I look happy?" Vincent said.

"No."

"I'm not. This isn't me. I'm a thug."

The woman named Peggy was tied to a chair. Vincent's orders were pretty straightforward. Jimmy owned an old house out in the middle of nowhere. He used it for out of town guests and used the basement for this sort of thing. Jimmy told Vincent to grab Peggy, take her to the house and take care of it.

And here they were in the clammy, dark basement. Taking care of it.

"I'm not used to this," Vincent said. "I get muscle jobs, because I'm so big, and I've got a mean face. I beat up smart alecks. I drive people around. I say 'Yes, sir' and 'No, sir' and 'Whatever you say, sir.' I'm a glorified yes-man. But now here I am, with you. I guess you could say this is a promotion. Do I look happy that I'm moving up?"

"No."

"I'm not a killer. I'm not an assassin. I'm a thug."

"I think you have my hands tied a little too tight," Peggy said.

"Excuse me?"

"And this chair is digging into my back."

"I could've just hog-tied you and thrown you on the floor, would that be better?"

"No," she said. "I'm fine. Thank you."

Now Vincent felt bad, Peggy seemed nice. Five foot four, short blonde hair, late thirties. Wholesome looking. She'd seemed very trusting when she opened her door to him, not a suspicion in the world until he grabbed her. The friendly type.

"What did you do anyway?" Vincent asked.

"Something I shouldn't have done."

Vincent looked at her. She smiled at him. "This is serious you know," he said.

"I know."

"You seem pretty calm about all of it."

Peggy shifted in the chair as much as she could. "Where's your gun?" she asked.

"I don't have one."

"No gun?"

"Jimmy gave me one once, but I didn't know how to take care of it. You have to clean those things, polish them. Load it, unload it, take it apart. It was too complicated." Vincent reached into his coat pocket and took out a folding knife. He'd only used it for threats before. He opened it and showed her the three-inch blade. It gleamed even though there was little light. "Now I just use this."

"Very nice."

"All I have to do is sharpen it every now and then, fold it up and stick it in my pocket. It's easier to take care of and a lot more reliable."

"They should put you in a commercial."

Vincent didn't understand her relaxed attitude. He folded the knife and put it back in his pocket. "Do you know what I'm supposed to do to you?" he asked.

"Yes."

"Aren't you scared?"

Peggy sat quiet for a moment. The cold walls seemed to close in. There must have been mold in the old basement;

Vincent's sinuses were itching. "I knew what I was doing," Peggy finally said. "I knew this would probably be the outcome. We should just get it over with."

"What did you do?" Vincent asked again.

Peggy didn't answer.

Vincent walked around the room. Cement walls with water stains here and there that he could barely see; one bare lightbulb hanging in the corner where it could do the least amount of good. Two support poles evenly spaced. He stopped in front of one of the water-stained walls to see if he could find a pattern in the marks like with clouds: a hand or a door or maybe a couch.

"Is there a problem?" Peggy asked behind him.

Vincent kept looking at the wall. "No, no problem."

He used to bounce at a bar down by the docks. He was great at it, never had to block a punch and never had to throw a punch. Most other bouncers, drunks wanted to try them. Not Vincent. Something about his look, his face, it stopped them. That was where Jimmy found him.

After going to work for Jimmy it was different. Vincent ended up in situations where punches had to be thrown. He maneuvered his hands so he didn't do too much damage. It was the beating that broke guys, not necessarily the pain. Still, it was nerve wracking trying to do the right thing in a wrong situation. Better pay but more guilt.

"If you're going to kill me, you're going to have to get a little bit closer."

Vincent turned to look at her. "This isn't exactly easy, you know. I never killed anybody before. I'm just a thug."

"If it makes you feel any better, I've never been killed before," Peggy smiled again. "So I guess that makes both of us new to this particular situation."

"What's wrong with you?" Vincent said. "This is serious!"

"You're thinking about it too much! Just put your knife against my throat and start slicing. Once you get started, you'll get the hang of it."

Vincent walked back over to Peggy. He stood behind the chair. "You think it's so easy?" he asked. "You think you could kill someone?"

Peggy sat a little straighter. "Sometimes I have this dream where I have three hands," she said. "Right hand. Left hand. Middle hand. It grows right out of my belly button. It's a weird dream, but I don't think it's a bad one. If I had three hands I could wear more jewelry. I love coloring my nails and a third hand would give me five more nails to paint. It would increase my hand-holding ability by fifty percent. I could hold more hands. It's not a bad dream. Then, when I wake up and see that I only have two hands, I'm sad."

"I don't understand."

"It's a dream," Peggy said. "There's nothing to understand. In a dream you're holding hands, when you wake up you're not."

"What are we doing here?" Vincent asked. "What did you do?"

Peggy didn't answer.

Vincent took the knife out of his pocket and opened in. The handle felt cool in his palm, like the chill of the room was seeping into the weapon.

He placed the blade against Peggy's neck.

Peggy's body tensed.

Vincent tried to move his hand. He couldn't.

Take care of it, Jimmy had said.

Vincent tried to slice. He couldn't.

This was a promotion. He was moving up.

Vincent tightened his grip on the knife. He tried to cut, to carve, to scratch. Anything.

Nothing.

He glanced at the wall, at the water stain. It still didn't look like anything.

"This isn't me," Vincent said. He took the knife away from Peggy's throat.

"Once a thug, always a thug," Peggy said. She sounded both relieved and disappointed.

As Vincent stepped away from the chair he folded the knife and put it back in his pocket. "I'm sorry."

"It's okay," Peggy said. "There are things certain people aren't cut out for. It's not your fault."

"Jimmy'll still get you. He'll just have somebody else take care of it."

Peggy smiled. Vincent noticed that she smiled a lot. "It's okay," she said again. "I've prepared myself. It wasn't easy, but I'm ready. I have people to see on the other side. I'm ready."

"What did you do?"

"Should I tell you?"

"Why not?"

Peggy was quiet for a moment. "I made a mistake," she said. "That's what I did. I made a bad mistake. But I don't regret it. Stephen and I were in this restaurant, this Chinese place."

"Who's Stephen?"

"My brother. We weren't saying much to each other, focused more on our food than anything else. Now, of course, I wish we'd been talking. Saying something, even arguing. Anything but that silence."

"They killed him?"

"These three men came in with guns. They opened fire. I guess Jimmy was mad at the owner for some reason, he sent three killers to take care of him. They did. They also took care of Stephen."

"I'm sorry."

"One thing about my brother and me, we never outgrew holding hands. We'd walk down the street hand in hand, just like when we were little. As soon as I put Stephen in the ground, I decided to find the men that killed him. I took care of them, all three of them."

The basement seemed to grow cooler. When Vincent exhaled he swore he could see his breath.

"I took my time while I did it," Peggy said. "They screamed. It's a very undignified way to die, screaming, begging for mercy. It's so degrading."

"But you're…"

"A middle-aged woman? And they were three strong men?"

"Yeah."

"I have my ways. One at a time all three of them screamed and bled and died. Then I disposed of the pieces."

Vincent walked over to the wall where he'd scrutinized the water stain. The air was making the itch in his head worse. He was disobeying orders. Not only was he not going to move up, he would probably be in even worse trouble. Orders were orders. Was he willing to buy this woman's life with his? He looked for the water stain and couldn't find it. It seemed to have evaporated.

"Jimmy'll still get you," Vincent said.

"If I stay alive," Peggy said, "Neither one of us gains anything."

Vincent took the knife back out of his pocket and slid it open.

"It's good that you're hesitant," Peggy said. "That apprehension means you're normal, you're human. I felt nothing."

Vincent moved back over to the chair.

"If I leave here alive," Peggy said, "I'll have to prepare to die all over again."

Vincent put the knife back to Peggy's throat. Time to prove he was more than a thug.

The Complete Pinscher

"I need the balls."

"I'm sorry. You need the…"

"The balls, the nuts, the testicles."

We were standing in one of Dr. Victor's examination rooms. Metal table, sink, wood cabinets, pet-sized scale, a box of tissues for when things didn't turn out well. The air smelled like bleach and sterilization.

"We don't…" Dr. Victor's eyebrows came together. "We dispose of them for you. It's all part of the procedure."

Ralph started whimpering and pulling on his leash. He had a white cone around his neck. He'd been here all day. He wanted to go home. "I don't want you to dispose of them for me. I want them."

"But… What on Earth for?"

"Not that it's any of your business," I said, "but someday Ralph is going to die. When that happens, I'm going to have him cremated. When I have him cremated, his balls are going with him."

Ralph was a black and tan Miniature Pinscher, somewhere in the neighborhood of three years old. I'd found him eating garbage in an alley on the north side of town. He was a scrawny thing and he smelled bad, but I felt like we were a good match for each other. I took him home and considered letting him keep his manhood, but having his balls chopped off was the right thing to do.

And now I wanted those balls.

Dr. Victor smiled at me like I just wasn't getting it. "We dispose of the medical waste for you."

"You said that. But they're mine. Or, they're Ralph's. And I want them."

Dr. Victor put on his serious face. "I'm afraid we're not able to do that. They need to be disposed of properly."

I put on my serious face. It was the same one I used when I spent my twenty-seven months in prison. It was much more serious than Dr. Victor's. "Put them into a jar of formaldehyde or something and I'll be on my way." Ralph started pulling harder on his leash. "Just a minute, boy."

Ralph whined.

"Mr. Karlecki, there are rules about this type of thing, laws. We have to…"

"Did you use a scalpel?" I asked. I didn't feel like talking about it anymore.

"For the procedure?"

"Yes."

"Yes. I used a scalpel. That's the easiest way. Some advancements have been made with lasers, but…"

I took my folding knife out of my jacket pocket. It had a mother of pearl handle and a three-inch blade. I pulled it open. "I'd use this," I said.

Dr. Victor swallowed. "You'd use that for…"

"For my procedure. On you."

"There's no need…I'm just…"

"I'm walking out of here with a pair of balls," I said. "They can be Ralph's or they can be yours."

Being inside takes something from you, something you can never get back. Time. Unmade memories. Hope. It's important to hold onto as much of yourself as possible.

When we got to the car, I put the bag the good doctor gave me into the back and lifted Ralph up onto the front seat. He was shivering even though it wasn't that cold. He tried to curl up, but had difficulty because of the cone. With the day, the cone and the procedure, he looked like he was miserable.

"Relax, boy," I said, stroking him between the ears. "It happens to all of us one way or another."

Daybreak

We used the sky to mark our time.

When the two of us went inside, the stars were at their deepest, filling the heavens with pinpricks of light. Now, as we came out, the sun was rising.

"This was…" I started.

"I know," Janet said. "I… I'd stay longer, but…"

I smiled. "If you stay any longer I might never let you leave."

She smiled back. I took her in my arms. I could still smell traces of her perfume from the night before. "Leave him," I said.

She tried to pull away from me. I didn't let her. She relaxed against my chest. "Tom, I love him."

"You love me, too."

"I do. But we've tried so many times. We fight. We hurt each other. It never works out."

We started in high school and we've carried on since. Even her wedding three years ago didn't stop us. Every few months her husband goes out of town and she comes back to me.

"We can try again," I said.

"No. This is the best it can be for us, me on one side of town with my life, you here with yours. The distance is good for us. It makes us work."

I knew she was right. I let her go. She got into her car and I watched her drive away. Something inside of me howled every time I watched her leave.

When I looked up at the sky for sympathy, the clouds looked back with red disdain.

The Last Croak

"Don't do this," Balthazar said, going down onto his knees on the grimy warehouse floor, his thick Cajun accent blurring his words. "I get you the money."

"You've been sayin' that," Colin said, taking the Ruger out of his coat pocket. "Mr. Walden is tired of waitin'."

"Think about this. If you let me live, I can work, I can earn, I can pay your boss back. If you shoot me, you never get the money. Surely he can see that!"

Joseph shook his head. "An example needs to be made for the other deadbeats."

"And you're it," Colin added.

"Don't do this," Balthazar repeated, defiance sneaking back into his voice. "If you do this, if you kill me, you will pay."

"Sure," Colin said. "We'll pay."

Joseph shook his head again.

"I curse you. As the seventh son of a seventh son, as a resident of the land where earth, water and magic meet, as a participant in all that is seen and all that is not seen, before I go to the dark I call the darkness within myself and curse the man that releases my spirit. I curse the man that sends me to the other side. I curse the man that..."

Colin pulled the trigger. In the empty warehouse, the gunshot sounded like a sharp, final laugh.

An hour later, Colin and Joseph were sitting at Joseph's kitchen table, each drinking a bottle of Bud Light Lime. A cassette of *Rust Never Sleeps* by Neil Young & Crazy Horse played on a boom box on the kitchen counter.

They couldn't think of anywhere better to go. Neither of them felt like sitting in a bar; when they did go out for a drink after a job was finished they both felt like everyone else in the bar was looking at them. If they went to a restaurant to get something to eat afterwards, they felt like everyone in the restaurant was looking at them. They spent a lot of time together as partners and as friends and a lot of that time was spent sitting around at Joseph's, were no one could look at them.

Neither Joseph nor Colin had said anything in the last six minutes. The smell of burnt toast lingered in the air from much earlier in the day. Joseph looked at his fingernails while Colin looked at his beer bottle.

Colin hiccupped.

Joseph looked up from his hand. "What's that?"

"I didn't say anything," Colin said. "I've got the hiccoughs."

"The hiccups."

"Hiccoughs, hiccups. Whatever."

"It bugs me when people call them hiccoughs," Joseph said.

"Fine. Hiccups." Colin hiccupped again.

"Thanks."

They sat in silence for another moment, Joseph looking back at his fingers and Colin looking at the scratched and stained surface of Joseph's wooden table.

Colin hiccupped again.

"I'm tired of doin' this," Joseph said.

"We could watch some TV," Colin said. "Or I could go home..."

"Not this. I mean the threats, the strong-arming people, the killing."

"I always do the killing."

"I know, and I appreciate that!"

"When did you ever kill anybody?"

"Never," Joseph agreed. "And I appreciate that! Believe me!"

"Then what's the problem?"

"I still have to be there. I still have to act like an asshole. I still have to help with the body."

Colin hiccupped.

"Honey-covered Christ!" Joseph said. "Drink some water or somethin'!"

"Maybe you should scare me."

"Right," Joseph said. He waved his hands in the air. "Boo!"

Colin smiled. "That guy tonight," he said, the smile leaving his face, "He was pretty scared."

"That's what I mean. The begging, the crying, a curse for Christ's sake! I don't like makin' people act like that, makin' them feel like that. I'm tired of it."

"Mr. Walden isn't gonna let you stop."

"I know that." Joseph took a drink of his beer. "I know."

"You're stuck."

"I suppose we both are." The song *Sail Away* came to an end and the cassette clicked to a stop. Joseph stood to turn the tape over. "I'm just tired of it."

Colin hiccupped. A deeper, darker, twisting, wrenching hiccup. With this exceptional auditory spasm, a greenish-brown blob shot out of Colin's mouth and landed on the table in front of him with a gaudy wet plop.

Joseph stood and looked at the blob.

Colin sat and looked at the blob.

After a second, the blob tried to hop away.

"Holy shit!" Colin screamed, jumping away from the table and knocking back his chair. "That's a frog!"

"Holy shit!" Joseph agreed.

"Holy fucking shit, a fucking frog just came out of my mouth!"

The frog reached the edge of the table, but couldn't seem to figure out how to get down to the floor.

"I could feel it," Colin said. "I could feel it squirmin' in my stomach, then wrigglin' up my chest, then crawlin' up my throat. I felt it come all the way up, burning and scratching. Holy shit, a fucking frog!"

Joseph crouched and took a closer look at the animal. "It might be a toad."

"What?"

"It might be a toad, not a frog."

"What's the difference!"

"Frogs tend to have smooth skin, while toads have more dry, bumpy skin. Frogs have teeth on the top of their mouths while toads don't have any teeth. Also, frogs are aquatic animals while toads live in wooded areas. Of course, if you want to get technical, toads are in the frog family, so, technically, toads are frogs."

"I meant," Colin said, "What's the difference as in *why does it fucking matter*? Whether it's a fucking toad or a fucking frog it doesn't change the fact that it just came out of my fucking mouth!"

"Right. I guess it doesn't matter."

Colin hiccupped and another frog splatted onto the table.

"Holy shit!"

"Holy shit!"

"Holy fucking shit, my insides are turning into frogs!" Colin said. "Take me to the hospital!"

The two frogs looked at each other on the table.

"Hold on, now..." Joseph said.

"Hold on now? Do you get what's happenin' here?"

"I do, but let's think about this..."

"Let's take me to the hospital!"

"What's going on here isn't natural."

"No, shit!" Colin agreed. "No, it isn't natural, it's not somethin' you hear about, but maybe I ate some frog eggs and now they're hatching. Or maybe I swallowed some water with tadpoles in it. Or... I don't know! But maybe a doctor can tell us what's goin' on!"

"I don't know."

Colin hiccupped and a third frog came up. This one landed on the kitchen floor.

"Holy shit!"

"It's the curse," Joseph said.

"What?"

"It's the curse," Joseph repeated.

Colin looked at him. The kitchen was starting to smell like stagnant water and dead vegetation. "You think that guy from earlier..."

"What was he, Cajun? Don't they have a lot of Voodoo down there in Louisiana"

"I suppose, but do you really think..."

"It makes more sense than you swallowin' tadpoles!"

"Then how come it's not happenin' to you?" Colin said. "You killed him, too."

Joseph thought for a moment. "No," he said. "I was just there. You pulled the trigger. He said somethin' about cursing the man that killed him, the man that sent him to the other side."

Colin pulled his chair forward and sat at the table in a daze. "That man was me."

One of the frogs croaked.

"I'm sorry, dude." Joseph sat back down, using his arm to brush the two table frogs onto the floor.

"How long do you think it'll last?"

"I don't know," Joseph said. "But, you did take that guy's life, so..."

"A life for a life."

"That would make sense."

Colin hiccupped and a fourth frog came up, landing on the kitchen table. Joseph brushed it away with his arm.

"Jesus that hurts! I feel like I'm being ripped apart."

"You want some Pepto Bismol?"

"I doubt that'll help." Colin's hand shook as he took a drink of his beer.

Joseph tried to look hopeful. "Maybe it's not for life, maybe it's just for a little while, then it'll go away."

"No," Colin said. "You were right, a life for a life. I can feel it. Maybe because it's me that the curse is on, but I know I'll be puking up frogs until the day I die."

"Maybe. But..."

Before Joseph could finish, Colin stood from the table and shambled into the living room, his right hand clutching his stomach as he walked. After a moment, he came back with his Ruger. He placed the gun on the table in front of Joseph. "I can't live like this," he repeated.

"What?"

"You have to take care of it. You have to take care of me."

"Wait..." Joseph stood, putting space between himself and the firearm. "I can't kill you."

"You have to."

"Maybe you were right," Joseph said. "Let's take you to the hospital."

"No. They can't do anything. That Cajun bastard knew how to place a curse."

"But..."

"You don't get it. It hurts. It hurts like nothin' else has ever hurt before. You have to end this for me."

Joseph picked up the gun and looked at it. He held the gun out to Colin. "Do it yourself."

"No. I can't."

"Try."

"I can't. I don't have it in me. You have to do it."

The air in the kitchen felt humid and close. "I've never..." Joseph said.

Colin gave three quick hiccups and a fifth, a sixth and a seventh frog came up, landing on the kitchen table. Colin moaned. The three animals looked up at him like he was their mother.

"Please?" Colin said, going down onto his knees on the kitchen floor, pain hitching his breath. "You don't know how it feels. My insides are being torn to pieces. I don't know how many more of these fucking reptiles I can stand."

"They're amphibians."

"Just fucking shoot me!"

Joseph picked up the gun. It felt warm in his hand and made his palm itch. He pointed it at Colin's head and curled his finger around the trigger. "I'm sorry."

Colin hiccupped. And eighth frog hit the floor. Blood trickled down Colin's chin.

"Holy fucking shit," Colin rasped. "Do it."

"What will I tell Mr. Walden?"

Colin looked up at him. "Tell him you're tired. That you quit. That you don't want to be an asshole anymore." Colin smiled. "And then get out of town."

"I'll do that," Joseph said, smiling back. Then he pulled the trigger. Blood and brains splattered the kitchen and Colin's body slumped to the floor.

"I'll tell him for both of us," Joseph said.

Trash Pick-Up

Frank Ryback woke to the sound of a garbage truck banging and clanging in the alley. Through the open bedroom window, the aroma of freshly turned trash drifted toward the bed. The blonde lying next to him didn't seem to mind the noise or the stench.

"Why do garbage men have to get up so early?" he asked her, sitting up and wiping sleep away from his face with a pink bed sheet.

She didn't respond.

His mouth tasted like asphalt and his head felt like a rubber band that was about to snap. Frank looked at his surroundings - the bedroom didn't seem familiar. They must've come back to her place. What was her name? Julie? Jasmine? Judith - yeah, that was it.

"You have a nice place here, Judith," he told her.

She didn't respond, she stayed face down on her pillow. In fact, she hadn't moved since the garbage collectors had yanked Frank out of dreamland.

He'd met her the night before at Puzzles Pub, a hole-in-the-wall bar in the hole-in-the-wall town of Currie Valley, Illinois. The tavern was down by the river and known for its All-You-Can-Eat-Spaghetti Night every Wednesday, it's slightly lopsided pool table and not much else.

Judith... was that it?... Wait, maybe it was Jasmine... Jasmine had been sitting at the bar alone, nursing a Bud Light. Her hair had an uncombed *I don't care* look and she seemed to be smiling at things that only she knew about.

Frank sat on the bar stool next to her, bought her another beer and hit her with as much charm as he could muster. The jukebox played *REO Speedwagon* and *Foreigner* like it was still 1986. They drank more beer, went out to the gravel parking lot and made out for twenty minutes, then went back inside and drank more beer. The evening started to get a little blurry at that point. They must have left Puzzles and come here, to Jasmine's apartment.

No... Julie. Not Jasmine. Not Judith. Her name was definitely Julie. They came back to Julie's apartment.

The garbage truck rumbled and backed up, beep-beep-beeping the entire way. The combination of noises hit Frank's ears like a sonic weapon.

Julie still didn't move.

Frank was starting to feel a little uncomfortable, sweat forming on his lower back, apprehension filling his thoughts. He hoped he hadn't done anything stupid last night. Every now and then he met ladies at bars and went home with them - sometimes he remembered the experience and sometimes alcohol prevented that luxury. As far as he knew he'd never done anything dangerous during one of these pick-ups, but he could be irritable. He got angry about little things every now and then. Once, in seventh grade, he lost his temper and stabbed his best friend with a pair of scissors over a McDonald's French fry.

What if last night something had upset him to the point of violence and he...?

He nudged Julie.

"Julie," he said. "You awake?"

She didn't respond.

"Julie?" He nudged her a little harder. "You okay? I didn't kill you, did I?"

Nothing. Julie didn't bat an eye.

This wasn't good. Frank gently rolled Julie onto her back. Her body was limp like a sock monkey. This really wasn't good. He put his hands on her shoulders, took a deep breath and shook her roughly.

"Wake up!" he yelled into her face. "Wake up! Don't be dead! Wake up!"

Julie came to life with a scream, terror etched on her face. Her hand shot under her pillow. When it came back out, morning light flashed on cold steel. She stabbed Frank in the stomach with the seven-inch Santoku knife from Paula Deen's Fourteen-Piece Stainless Steel Kitchen Knife Set.

Frank slumped onto the bed.

"I'm sorry!" she said, confusion on her face, then panic. "I'm sorry! I keep it under my pillow in case of burglars! I sleep so deep! When I wake up, I just... I don't know... I just... You frightened me! I'm sorry."

"Julie..." Frank said, blood pouring from the wound. "Call an ambulance..."

As Frank Ryback faded away to nothingness, he heard her ask, "Julie? Who's Julie?"

Dancing on the Edge of Darkness

The waltz was slow, but it was disappearing quickly.

The music flowed over them like the current in a river of remembrance. Each step was a memory of their short life together. In many ways, it was torture. It was also the best, most peaceful moment they would ever know.

Greg and Roberta Larson were newly-weds. They were on their honeymoon. They were in bungalow number three at the Lover's Lane Roadside Cottages. They were on their way to Niagara Falls.

This was supposed to be the beginning of their forever.

A little over a year ago, they met at a wedding reception. Mutual friends were tying the knot. Neither one of them was with anybody, so they danced together all night. They were two people with unremarkable features, him a little tall, her a little short, but her blond hair went perfectly with his blue eyes. At the end of the evening, he asked for her phone number.

"Where are we going?" she asked when, one week later, he picked her up for their first date.

"It's a surprise. Close your eyes."

She played along. They talked as he drove. She couldn't see that he wasn't watching the road. He was too busy looking at the way her hair fell in her face.

He pulled the car to a stop. "Okay," he told her.

She opened her eyes and grinned at the Burger King sign.

"It's not the golden arches," he said, "but I figure we can work our way up to that. It *is* just our first date."

"Will you get me anything I want?"

"Anything."

"Three Whopper Value Meals."

"With cheese?"

"With *extra* cheese."

She ate everything and then ordered a chocolate shake. His pretend shock couldn't hide his smile.

The waltz continued.

Three months ago, they took dancing lessons. They wanted to be ready for their own wedding reception. They learned how to tango and rumba and swing. Their favorite dance was the waltz; they thought it was the most romantic.

Their wedding ceremony was a simple affair with a few chosen relatives and a few special friends. The reception, however, was the event that Greg and Roberta had looked forward to. They invited everyone they'd ever met: high school classmates, college friends, co-workers and relative after relative after relative. It was a party to celebrate their love with food, music and, of course, dancing.

How long? How long in the darkness of night had they been shifting their bodies to the sluggish tune? How long had they been moving as one, his face buried in her neck, her flesh catching his tears? This dance had to last an eternity, but it was taking only insufficient seconds.

"Let's wrap it up," said a voice from the shadows.

They'd registered earlier that evening. "Larson," Greg had told the check-in clerk.

"Mr. And Mrs.," Roberta added. "It's our first night as a married couple."

"Terrific," the clerk said, sounding almost like he meant it. He registered the happy twosome, then led them to their cottage. A thin pink bedspread was pulled over a lumpy mattress; a cracked mirror hung in the bathroom and amateur paintings of the seaside drooped from the walls. They were delighted at how shabby the cabin was.

"It's not the Hilton," Greg said, "but it *is* just our first night as husband and wife."

As soon as they were out of their formal clothes, Mr. And Mrs. Larson went to bed. They did the things that married people do, then they fell asleep.

Around midnight, there was a knock at the cabin door. Bleary eyed and still bursting with joy, Greg opened it.

Three men forced their way into their Honeymoon Suite. They carried guns.

"We need a place to hide for a few hours," the leader of the criminals said. His breath smelled like mouthwash.

"Don't hurt us," Greg said.

"We wouldn't think of it."

"It's our first night as a married couple," Roberta added.

"That's real sweet."

Hiding didn't work, the police found the runaways. Now everyone was dealing with something they didn't want to deal with: a hostage situation.

They were both scared, but Greg did his best to keep Roberta calm. He made faces whenever the fugitives weren't looking and Roberta smiled, trying to look like everything would be all right.

Time didn't move. The outlaws, whoever they were, whatever they'd done, were getting restless.

"The cops aren't giving in. It's time to set an example."

They decided on him. She cried. He said not to worry. They pulled him to the door, gun pointed at his chin.

"One last dance," Greg said.

It was a strange desire, but the bandits were gracious. They would grant a dying man his last request.

Mr. Larson joined Mrs. Larson in the center of the room. His hands went to her waist, her arms rested on his shoulders. There was no music, but it didn't matter. They both remembered the music from their wedding, from their first dance as husband and wife. The outlaws watched from the sides of the room.

This was supposed to be a time to take pictures and make memories and enjoy all of the movements and events that marriage had promised, a time for dreams and expectations. It was supposed to be a time to plan for what was to come. Instead, it was their last moment together. Holding onto each other, never wanting to let go. Swaying to silent music in a run-down motel.

One of the bandits pulled Greg and Roberta Larson apart.

The music stopped.

A gun fired.

The waltz was over.

Acknowledgements

Terry Tenderloin and the Pig Thief
First published in *Shotgun Honey*, June 21, 2013

The Resurrection at Hasenpfeffer Field
First published on the author's blog, *Captain Spaulding on Skull Island*, December 15, 2009

Lucky
First published in *Shotgun Honey*, April 24, 2015

Long Distance Rumbles
First published in Issue 7 of *Bullet*, November 2006

Alleyway Alvin
First published in *Out of the Gutter*, October 8, 2017

Sunset Requiem
First published in *Hardluck Stories*, March 2004

Mama's Drapes
First published in *The Clarity of Night*, April 19, 2007

A Night For Chicken Pizza
First published in *Shotgun Honey*, October 5, 2020

Larcenous Zydeco
First published in *Kings River Life Magazine*, March 14, 2020

Blue Bullet Waltz
First published in *Pulp Metal Magazine*, October 7, 2011

Words Fall Like Nothing
First published in *Shotgun Honey*, May 30, 2011

In Lieu of Crimson Roses
First published in *Every Day Fiction*, November 15, 2007

Devotion and the Autumn Chill
First published in Volume 1, Number 3 of *Mount Zion Speculative Fiction Review*, 2007

Sparrows & Crows
First published in *Crime Factory*, October 2010

Long Black Gloves
First published in *A Twist of Noir*, October 2011

Breaking
First published in *ASSA*, 2008

Like Sapphires in the Sea
First published in *Hardluck Stories*, March 2007

The Thug and the Three-Handed Lady
Original to this collection

The Complete Pinscher
First published in *Shotgun Honey*, March 26, 2012

Daybreak
First published in *The Clarity of Night*, November 7, 2007

The Last Croak
First published in *Shotgun Honey Presents: Reloaded*, September 10, 2013

Trash Pick-Up
First published in *Near To The Knuckle*, September 24, 2015

Dancing on the Edge of Darkness
First published in the anthology *Family Gatherings*, June 2003

About the Author

Once upon a time, *Locus* Magazine called John Weagly "a new writer worth reading and following." His short stories have been nominated for the Derringer Award multiple times, winning one in 2008, and various other accolades. As a playwright, 100 of his scripts have received over 150 productions on four continents and have been featured in the curriculum at Columbia College. He lives in Chicago with his girlfriend and many animals.